NEW BEGINNINGS IN DREAM VALLEY

VALLEY

A SWEET FEEL-GOOD ROMANCE

S J CRABB

ALSO BY S J CRABB

The Diary of Madison Brown

My Perfect Life at Cornish Cottage

My Christmas Boyfriend

Jetsetters

More from Life

A Special Kind of Advent

Fooling in love

Will You

Holly Island

Aunt Daisy's Letter

The Wedding at the Castle of Dreams

My Christmas Romance

Escape to Happy Ever After

Cruising in Love

Coming Home to Dream Valley

Christmas in Dream Valley

New Beginnings in Dream Valley

sjcrabb.com

NEW BEGINNINGS IN DREAM VALLEY

When Eliza Benson saw a job advertised on her way to work, she couldn't believe her luck.

Writer requires a live-in assistant for six months to assist with admin and housekeeping duties.

It came at the perfect time because she was desperate to ditch her dreary life in London as a legal secretary and start over.

Despite her mother's horror at the thought of her only child living with a stranger, Eliza took the position and headed to the small town of Dream Valley to meet her new employer, who turned out to be the darling of daytime television, actor Bill Monroe.

It was all going to plan until Eliza realised she had none of the qualities needed. As it turns out, faking your CV to get a job has repercussions. How could she be the perfect housekeeper when she couldn't even boil water?

With the help of the locals, Eliza began a crash course in all things domestic in a bid to stay.

Then Bill's wife and son arrived, and Eliza discovered she had been set up and his family had an ulterior motive for her employment.

Lurching from one crisis to another, Eliza is determined to show she is more than capable and despite hating Bill's controlling, dominant son Blake on sight, she is soon involved in a deception of the most complicated kind.

Can Eliza prove she can boil water with ease and excel at all things domestic, and will Bill ever discover the lengths his family have gone to on his behalf?

Set in Dream Valley, a small-town set by the sparkling sea, and home to a cast of crazy characters, Eliza and Blake find more than they bargained for.

PROLOGUE

SOMEWHERE FAR AWAY FROM DREAM VALLEY

*T*he rain hasn't stopped all morning and just the gentle drip of the drops collecting in the bucket reminds me I really need a new job, and fast.

Sighing, I look out of the window and watch the droplets of water running down the windowpane, matching my mood perfectly.

This is it. My life. Resigned to watching rain fall, one step away from watching paint dry.

"Miss Benson, a word, please."

Startled, I look up as my manager, Mr Henderson, there are no christian names in Pemberley Thompson, frowns down at me.

The fact he has elevated his desk onto some kind of stage in the office means he's always looking down at the workers beneath him. Not that he needs it because he does that with his supercilious expression, anyway.

"Your report is late, and you are staring out of the window as if the answer lies there. Do we have a problem, Miss Benson, because the clock is ticking?"

Forcing myself to smile, in a professional way, of course, I nod. "I'm sorry, Mr Henderson, the report will be on your desk by close of business."

"I take it you mean, close of business today, Miss Benson, because I'm afraid you can't leave until it is. The client is counting on our professionalism in this matter and our reputation is at stake."

"Understood, Mr Henderson."

He turns away and positions himself behind his desk, keeping his eagle eyes on me as I bend my head to my work, feeling like a modern-day Bob Cratchit. At least that's what it feels like.

I can't recall how many months I've spent at Pemberley Thompson, but I know one thing: I need to leave for my own sanity.

I have been an assistant in a family run solicitors for too long already and aside from Mr Henderson, the only person closest in age to me is Miss Travers, who works the same job as I do. The fact that she's thirty years my senior means we don't have a lot in common and I can see myself in her shoes when she's long since retired. I will *be* Miss Travers unless I do something about it, which brings me back to the reason for my daydream in the first place.

The job application.

I saw it on my way to work this morning as I scrolled through the job adverts on my phone.

WRITER REQUIRES LIVE-IN ASSISTANT FOR SIX MONTHS TO ASSIST WITH ADMIN AND HOUSEKEEPER DUTIES.

The pay is more than I earn here in a year, and it sounds so tempting. I could work for six months and then take six months to find another job. This could be just the break I need, except for one niggling little doubt that just won't go away.

The live-in part.

I mean, I'm not averse to trying new things but to head off to live with a man, at least I think it's a man, in a strange place for six months, screams murdering psychopath. If my mother even knew I was thinking of it, she would have a heart attack and for every reason why I should go, a hundred other reasons why I shouldn't are screaming at me.

"Miss Benson."

Mr Henderson barks my name like a sergeant major and I jump as he drives his fist down on the desk.

"I will not tell you again—work!"

Pushing away the job dream, at least until my train journey home, I sigh and turn my attention to the last will and testament of Annalise Turtle.

* * *

ANNALISE TURTLE STAYS with me as I grab my coat and umbrella from the hook on the door. Turn my back on an office that drains the life from my soul every second I spend there and head out onto the busy pavement outside and start the commute home with several thousand other people who are in this rat race with me.

Is this really my life? Annalise Turtle would think me a fool. Despite how arduous my job is, I come across a superstar sometimes and none that shines as bright as Annalise did when she was alive.

She lived alone in a huge mansion by the looks of things. Her property portfolio is admirable, and her art collection is currently on its way to Christies. She had it all, bar one thing. A family. There were many admirers, as my mum would say. I like to think of them as lovers.

Picturing her rather hedonistic lifestyle, drifting from Monte Carlo one month to the Caribbean the next, a different companion each time, makes me long for a life like that. I bet she never watched rain drip down the windowpane. She would probably run outside and dance in it. Yes, Annalise Turtle had the right idea, and the fact she amassed her great fortune by marriage doesn't even matter to me. A steady stream of ex-husbands. The longest lasting just two years and the shortest a few weeks. A gold digger of the most successful kind, who finally enjoyed her wealth by relishing the company of young men with the same idea as she had. But she was shrewd and never married them. Preferring to play the field instead and enjoy her hard-earned fortune.

No, Annalise Turtle wasn't content with normal, ordinary, or boring. She wanted it all and I should take a leaf out of her crowded little black book and do something unconventional for the first time in my life before I turn thirty.

I'm going to apply for that job as soon as I get home.

CHAPTER 1

*S*omebody should have talked me out of this. What was I thinking? A moment of madness could be the ruin of me because I have agreed to live with a strange man in an unfamiliar place, far away from home and everybody who knows me.

I am currently locked in a cab, travelling to a weird place called Dream Valley that must surely be somebody's idea of a joke. Mind you, it's exactly what appealed to me when I saw the job advert on my phone. It shouted of new beginnings, fresh starts, and a place where dreams come true, and I could reinvent myself, which is probably long overdue. Having worked at Pemberley Thompson since I left college, I was resigned to a lifetime of tedium running the race with the other rats in the city. London is a far cry from Dream Valley and that's a very good thing.

The bright lights of the capital no longer hold any appeal for me. There is no fun in waking in the early hours in the suburbs and joining a packed train where seats are always in short supply. Travelling to a city that could use a good clean and trades on its history. Don't get me wrong, there is something extremely exciting about London. A big city where anything could happen and a link to the past that many never get the measure of.

I'm not sure when it lost its appeal, but for many years now I've existed, not lived and it took reading about the amazing life of another to strike the match on my own destiny.

"Where are you from?"

The cheery voice of the taxi driver rouses me from my deliberations, and I say brightly, "Kent, near Whitstable on the north coast."

"Can't say I've ever been there."

"It's quite pretty, really." Thinking about home makes me feel worried all over again. What am I thinking, ditching the safe and secure for wild abandon? I don't even know this man and here I am, heading his way on a wing and a prayer.

"What's taking you to Dream Valley?"

He persists with his questions, and I wonder how best to answer them. Do I put it out there that I'm a fool, or do I make out I have it all worked out and in charge of my life?

"A new job."

"Ah, a new beginning. That sounds exciting."

"I couldn't have put it better myself."

I chuckle to myself because he's right about that. A new beginning for a life that's reached stalemate. I've been moving sideways for so long now I've forgotten what it's like to make an actual decision. Going with the flow and doing the expected. Now it's time for the unexpected to have its turn and as I peer out of the slightly steamy window, I wonder about where I'm going. I've googled it, of course I have, but it didn't really tell me much except it's a place where not a lot happens. Well, nothing that's made it to the internet. No scandals, murders or history, from what I could gather, and I wonder about my choice of a fresh start. Mind you, it had nothing to do with the location and everything to do with the man.

Bill Monroe. Middle-aged actor who has graced most

daytime screens for a decade in the hugely popular hospital drama, Emergency Room. Doctor Ralph Deneres is the chief surgeon and has dealt with crisis on repeat, as well as a very turbulent love life. It's my mother's favourite show and she even records it to watch in peace when nobody is around to interrupt her. Although the house stands empty for much of the day, she hates it when anybody disturbs her salivating over the desirable good doctor.

"So, what is this amazing new beginning you have waiting for you?"

Once again, I'm plucked from my thinking time and say with a hint of nerves, "A job. I answered an advert for a live-in assistant. It's a bit worrying, really."

He whistles, which doesn't make me feel any better about my decision.

"Well, you're certainly brave living on the job. I hope you like it when you're there."

"Oh, it will be fine." I dismiss his concerns as if they hadn't already occurred to me several times a day and often in the night when I wake in a cold sweat, agonising over my poorly judged life choice.

"If I hate it, I'll leave. Maybe you have a business card you can give me in case I'm in need of a quick getaway."

I laugh as if I'm joking, but I am more than serious.

"Sure, I quite like thinking of myself as a knight in shining armour."

He chuckles to himself and as I look out at the countryside racing past, I feel my heart heavy with worry. It all seemed like such a good idea at the time. Answer an ad to prise me from my comfort zone and force me to face up to the fact my life is going absolutely nowhere. I am wasting the best years of my life tucked away in a dimly lit office that's definitely seen better days, doing the kind of work that sucks the will to live from me like one of Harry Potter's Death Eaters. I want more. I always have and it's the perfect time to ditch the familiar and plunge headfirst into new beginnings, as the taxi driver calls it. This could be the making of Eliza Benson. I certainly hope so because if it's not, I'll be crawling back to Pemberley Thompson on my hands and knees and begging for mercy and my old job back.

Dull skies and drizzle are replaced by blue skies and sunshine, and it reaffirms that I made the right decision. There is no congestion, no honking of horns and no traffic lights. Just a long, winding road through the most perfect countryside, flanked by lush green fields with only sheep and cows for company.

I'm guessing the air is crisp and pure and not containing high levels of carbon emissions and God only knows what else.

Sinking back in my seat, I congratulate myself on my bravery because if I didn't, nobody else would.

"What does your family think about your new job?"

Once again, the driver cuts in and must be psychic because I was thinking back on when I told my mum I was leaving for pastures new.

"You're doing what?" Her incredulous, rather high-pitched voice rang in my ears as she stared at me with horror.

"You can't be serious, Eliza. What are you thinking?" I watched her pace around the kitchen while throwing me disbelieving looks.

"You could be murdered, raped and imprisoned for all I'd know."

"Don't be so dramatic, mum."

I remember rolling my eyes as she said in horror, "I am losing my mind here, young lady. Just wait until your father hears about this. I'm not sure I can help you on this occasion."

She carried on pacing and shaking her head as if she couldn't believe what she just heard.

"This is so out of character, love, it just isn't you. Are you on drugs? It would certainly explain it. Was it somebody on the train, a dealer perhaps? It must be narcotics that have confused your brain because I didn't raise you to make impetuous life-threatening decisions like this."

"I'm not on drugs, mum." It made me laugh, which angered her further. "Do you think this is a joke, Eliza, because I can assure you, I'm not laughing? This smacks of some weird pervert luring an attractive girl into his home to imprison her and make her his sex slave. Oh no, I'm sorry I forbid it. Absolutely not. It's not going to happen. What on earth possessed you to apply in the first place?"

She looked at me as if I was a stranger inhabiting her daughter's body and I still remember how good it felt when I played my winning card.

"Because I want to do something with my life."

"You are. You're working and making your own way in the world. You know, like the rest of mankind."

"But it's not what I want to continue doing – I want more."

Mum threw up her hands in exasperation. "We all want more, Eliza, but sometimes you have more than enough already. Life isn't like a rom com, you know. Real life is hard, demanding, and requires dedication. We can't all ditch everything we've worked for and head off into the sunset, hoping to find a better life. It doesn't work like that. I should know, I married your father."

"What's that supposed to mean?" I am genuinely confused, and she fixes me with a despairing look and sighs. "Don't you think I wanted more? Well, I did. I wanted someone dashing and adventurous. Somebody who would sweep me off my feet and carry me around the world on adventures. We've all wished for that young lady, but there comes a time when we accept that this is as good as it gets. You're lucky if you can afford a foreign holiday half the time and if you start a family, you may as well say goodbye to any hopes and dreams you had for yourself because they take precedent over anything *you* want."

"Then now is the perfect time."

"There *is* no perfect time. You certainly shouldn't be entertaining fanciful thoughts about throwing in a good job and taking off to… where was it again?"

"Dream Valley."

"Oh, for god's sake, Eliza, it's worse than I thought. Let me see. London and a good job, or Dream Valley and a psychopath. I wonder what the best thing would be?"

"Dream Valley." I stared at her with a determined look, and she snorted. "For goodness' sake, grow up Eliza, and face the facts. This is your best life already — enjoy it before your looks fade, your metabolism deserts you and your health gives out. Make the most of being single in London, but not too much. I do want a grandchild or two and you're not getting any younger."

"Aren't you even going to ask me what the job involves?"

I still remember that feeling when I stared her in the eye as she placed her hands on her hips and said with a roll of her eyes, "Ok, what is this amazing opportunity that involves putting your safety on the line and giving up everything you've ever worked for?"

"I'd be the live-in assistant of Bill Monroe, aka Dr Ralph Deneres."

Still chuckling to myself, I remember the shocked look on her face and, for the first time in my life, my mother was speechless. She looked at me as if I had grown two heads and had lost the power of speech. I remember how good it felt that I had stopped her in her tracks for the first time in my life and then witnessed a complete about turn in a matter of seconds.

Her face brightened and the smile that took over was quite comical to watch.

"Are you kidding me?" Expressions of envy mixed with euphoria flitted across her face and she rubbed her hands together in glee. "*My* Doctor Deneres, from Emergency Room?"

Her face was flushed and her eyes bright as she completely came down on my side.

There was no more talk of rash decisions and ruining my life. There were no harsh words or recriminations. Instead, there was nothing but advice and congratulations as my mother did a complete about turn and started planning the rest of my life out on the spot, which involved her spending a lot of quality time with my new gorgeous, (in her words) boss.

CHAPTER 2

he taxi starts to slow down, and I look out at the scene that has changed from open countryside to include the ocean. A beautiful, sparkling sea of happiness that lifts my spirits and makes everything better. It feels as if I'm on the edge of the world and free of the chains of normal life. I can be anything here and I long to reinvent myself as a free spirit and a woman who takes adventure as her middle name. Gone is the old Eliza Benson. The one who did as she was told and played the long game. I am now officially reincarnated with the spirit of Annalise Turtle, and I can do anything in life I want.

"Nice place." The taxi driver sounds impressed, and I can see why, because we are heading to the end of the road. The point of no return, where the only move to make is a U turn because there is no way forward from here.

Rock House sits on a headland jutting out to sea and is the only destination on this piece of land. We head through large electric gates that close behind us and as we drive slowly up the magnificent driveway, I catch my breath because this is way more than I expected.

Secluded paradise. That's the only way I can describe it and as the house rears up in front of us, all glass and modern luxury, I blink twice as I imagine spending a very happy few months as lady of all I survey.

The car stops at the entrance and the taxi driver turns and smiles. "That will be thirty pounds please, miss."

Rummaging in my purse, I draw out the crisp notes that were brand new from the cash machine and handing him an extra five pounds for the tip, I smile gratefully.

"Thank you so much."

He pockets the cash and nods. "Any time. You've got my number safe, haven't you?"

Fingering the white card, I smile. "Safe and sound."

As I open the door, I step out into the sunlight and take deep cleansing breaths of the fresh sea air. This is what I needed. Oxygen, solitude, and space to breathe. Perfect in every way and so far, so good. This is just what I pictured in my mind, and I can't wait to explore further.

The taxi driver heaves my cases from the boot of the car and places them on the stone step that is set before an amazing wooden door, painted in a light shade of grey.

"Would you like me to wait until you get inside?"

He cocks his head towards the door, and I smile nervously. "Would you mind?" I'm grateful for the offer because what if mum's right and the man's a monster? At least I could size him up in a few seconds flat and make a quick getaway. It would be annoying, but at least I'd be alive.

Tentatively, I ring the doorbell and hear it chime loudly in the hallway inside. Listening eagerly for any sign of life, I relax a little when I hear footsteps heading my way.

As the door opens, I see a man that requires no introduction because I have googled the hell out of him, not to mention watched every single one of mum's recorded episodes that she insisted on watching with me, in the name of research. I had to admit he was rather gorgeous in an 'older man' sort of way. Salt and pepper hair with stunning blue eyes, set in a chiselled face with a strong jaw. A nice-looking body that was flaunted from every angle the camera invented and a kind expression that makes you want to divulge every secret you've got.

"You must be Eliza." He holds out his hand and I shake it tentatively. "Good afternoon, sir."

"Call me Bill, sir is so formal."

He glances past me to the taxi driver, who is looking at him with awed excitement, and he smiles. "How much do I owe you?"

"The lady paid already." The driver stutters a little and it's obvious he's just as starstruck as my mother, and shaking his head, Bill pulls out a wallet from his pocket and counts out five ten-pound notes. "Refund the lady and take this instead, I insist."

Without even missing a beat, the driver thrusts my money back at me and pockets the celebrity cash instead and looks at me with understanding dawning in his eyes. It almost feels as if he approves, which makes me feel a lot better about the choice I just made. I'm slightly amused to see him back away as if from royalty and I say quickly, "Um, thank you."

He waves as he enters his cab and as he starts the engine, Bill reaches down and grabs my two cases. "Come on in and I'll make you a cup of tea, or something stronger if you prefer. We can discuss the job in more detail when we're more comfortable."

I don't even look for any hidden messages behind those words because there is no way in hell this man is anything but genuine. In fact, he could ask me to divulge every secret I have, and I would do so gladly because Bill Monroe is every bit as charismatic as the man he plays on screen.

He leaves my cases in the hallway and I follow him through a large open plan room into the kitchen. There is nothing not to like about this house. Light, modern, and tasteful. Nothing out of place and the perfect space to unwind and contemplate life.

We pass through a large living area with super fabulous views of the ocean and I love the bifold doors that appear to be a feature. The kitchen is no different and sleek modern appliances and cabinets make it a chef's dream. I hear the call of seagulls from the open door and feel the breeze calm my heated skin. Inwardly, I relax because this is turning out to be a dream come true and nothing like I imagined it would be.

"So, Eliza, I must start by thanking you for trusting an old pro and agreeing to live with me for as long as it takes."

He slides a mug towards me with a wink. "I made coffee. I'm useless with tea and don't have anything else until the food delivery turns up tomorrow."

"Tomorrow."

He nods. "I thought we'd grab a takeaway or eat out tonight and get to know one another. I'm sure you have many questions and I'm happy to answer them as best I can."

As I sip my tea, I watch him from underneath my lashes because this feels so strange. I'm sitting drinking coffee with a famous actor and to say I'm a little overawed by this situation, is putting it mildly.

He takes the seat opposite me at the breakfast bar and smiles. "So, first up, just to reassure you and put your mind at ease, I need someone who will keep me alive. Feed me, wash my clothes, and bring me endless coffee. Take any calls on my behalf and relate the important ones back to me. Make sure the place is tidy and visitors turned away. I want total solitude for however long it takes to write my screenplay, and I have taken a sabbatical to focus on the job."

He fixes me with an eager look. "The rest of your time is your own. Read, watch tv, explore the area, do whatever you like. I'll be tied up with writing most days and would just like company in the evenings on the odd occasion and someone to prevent me from going stir crazy. I know it's a lot to ask being holed up with an old man like me, but I hope you won't hold it against me."

"Of course not. I can't wait to start."

Taking a sip of my coffee, I wonder why he needs to pay

someone to be his companion when my google search revealed he is most definitely married with a family of his own.

He must be a mind reader because he says with a grin, "You must be wondering why?"

"It did cross my mind." Throwing him an apologetic smile, he runs his fingers through his hair and sighs. "I love my family, too much sometimes, but on this occasion, I need distance from them if I am ever going to finish this project. You see, my wife Julia is rather energetic and there doesn't appear to be an 'off' switch. My son Blake is a busy successful man who appears irritated by everyday life and clashes terribly with his mother, and evenings at home are a little volatile, to put it mildly. So, I came up with this great idea to squirrel myself away somewhere far from home and grab some much-needed peace and quiet."

He grins impishly and now I know why he is so adored by so many. He is a very likeable, sexy man and if he was a little younger, I would be as intoxicated with him as my mother is.

But he has a son, and that little gem hasn't gone unnoticed, and I say casually, "So, your son still lives with you?"

He raises his eyes and I see a slight twinkle in them that causes me to giggle. "I mean, you said he was successful. I thought he may have his own place…"

I'm feeling a little flustered as I delve into his private life and Bill groans. "I wish. He likes all the comforts of home and treats it like a hotel. He did move out for a short time, but soon came running back when it wasn't to his liking. He's a stockbroker in the city and keeps exhausting hours. I suppose he struggled to fend for himself and works so hard, it was easier to come home to Wimbledon every night instead. He's no fool and the way his mother fusses around after him, I'm doubtful he will ever leave and so I'm doing it instead. Placing myself out of harm's way for some brief solitude and just hope they don't figure out a way to get here easily."

"So, you won't be seeing them for the duration." I'm a little shocked about that, and he groans. "I doubt I will be that lucky. No, I'm guessing once they work out a route down here, they'll be pounding down the door, which is why I need you to be a dragon."

My mouth drops and he grins. "Keep them away from me and do your best to distract them."

He leans his elbows on the smooth marble surface and places his chin in his hand. Just the intense look he gives me makes me squirm a little, and he says with a sigh, "If it was that easy, I'd just stay here alone and exist on takeaways, but I'm not a fool. Julia will soon become unbearable, and Blake will bring her to me just to get some peace himself. I'm guessing in less than a week they'll arrive at the door, and he'll leave her here and head back for some alone time. However..." he laughs out loud. "He'll soon miss her meals, housekeeping service and fussing and realise that fending for oneself is not all it's cracked up to be. Then he'll head back to claim her and so it will go on for the entire time we're here."

"It sounds exhausting."

He nods. "That's why I'm paying you so well. Danger money." He winks and in this moment I would do absolutely anything for Bill Monroe because I don't think I have ever liked anyone on sight as much as I do the friendly man before me. Thinking of my own family, probably booking their visit already, I wonder if I'm up to this job. Perhaps I should admit defeat in advance and head off with my bags remained unpacked and my tail between my legs.

CHAPTER 3

$\mathcal{B}$ ill takes me on a tour of the house and surroundings, and I'm amazed at how quickly I've already fallen in love with Rock House and Dream Valley. Its picture postcard perfect and the stuff of dreams, like the name suggests.

The house itself is chic elegance with no frills, just minimalism at its best. Bill showed me to an annexe attached to the main house where I will be staying. Close enough for practicalities and far enough to enable me some privacy of my own. I was secretly glad about that because I had been worried about meeting him on the landing after a mad dash to the bathroom and thought things could have got awkward. This way our lines are divided, and I can relax knowing I have my own space that's unlikely to be invaded when I least expect it.

His own space is like something out of Homes and Gardens. Beautifully decorated and a real home from home. Thinking of his lifestyle in London, I'm guessing success brings great riches and I remember the spread in OK Magazine where it was featured. His wife was attractive as expected and appeared kind and sweet. Even in the photographs it was apparent he idolises her and the way he held her hand and looked at her with proud delight, made me relax knowing he seemed ok. Not weird at all and I am already congratulating myself on my best decision in life.

The inside of this property may be amazing, but the outside is breath-taking. Doors that open onto a large space overlooking the sea. The only onlookers are just a curious seagull or two because Rock House lies in perfect solitude and only the roar of the ocean disturbs a serene paradise.

"Impressive, isn't it?"

Bill's voice holds an excitement that mirrors my own, and I nod vigorously. "It's amazing. How did you find it?"

"A friend of mine stayed here last summer. He told us about it, and I made a mental index note to revisit it as a potential bolt hole. I had my agent liaise with the owners and arrange a long term let because it's normally booked out for short breaks and holidays, so it took some juggling."

"How long have you booked it for?"

"Six months." He laughs softly. "I doubt I'll get that long, but I planned the worst-case scenario."

For a moment, he looks concerned. "Six months contract was the agreement. Is that still ok with you?"

I squint into the distance, wishing I'd worn my shades and say with a nod. "Yes, it's perfect. It allows me enough time to work things out and gives me the resources to take my time in considering what I want to do next."

"So, you're at a turning point; a junction."

"I think I am." I turn and smile. "For years, I've played the usual game. Worked hard, found a good job that pays well and thought I was doing the right thing. Like your son, I still live at home, which is not a good look for a soon to be thirty-year-old. It took reading about another person's adventurous life to point me in the right direction. Open my eyes and take a good look at my own one and this position was advertised at the opportune moment."

I watch his shoulders relax as he nods, deep in thought. "I think we may be at that same junction, Eliza. Change is a part of life nobody likes. It's so easy to stick with the familiar, plod along and enjoy the small successes that keep you in line. Many people thought I was mad to request a sabbatical from Emergency Room, my own family included. They were concerned the public would forget about me the moment my face left the screen, and the press wasn't stalking my every move. Professional suicide, my agent called it, but I took the plunge, anyway."

"Does that scare you?" I'm curious because it's becoming clearer by the second that we share something huge in common and I wonder if he's feeling the same and he grins, an infectious twinkle in his eye that makes me smile. "Hell, yeah. This is the scariest thing I've ever done, but I'm loving every second of it. New beginnings are the best kind, wouldn't you say? At the moment, we are both standing here facing an unknown future. We have six months to steer our lives in a direction we'd rather be going or admit defeat and head back the way we came, knowing we tried at least. Many don't even reach it this far, so it's up to us to make it count. You will discover your destiny or at least enjoy a nice break for a few months, and I will either discover a whole new direction for my career, or head back to Emergency Room, hopefully in a blaze of glory. Sometimes a break is just what's needed, and my adoring public will be glad I'm back. I'm the lucky one I guess, because I am stepping aside, not backwards and haven't yet started the descent from the top of the mountain. I'm just taking time to enjoy the view."

He smiles and then looks at his watch.

"I'm sorry. I can send an insomniac to sleep with my ramblings. You must be tired from your journey and want to settle in. I'll leave you to it and make a start on my screenplay. I am itching to do it, and so please can I ask you to come and find me in a couple of hours with a cup of coffee and some digestives? Don't be afraid to knock, either. I won't bite your head off."

He turns and I say quickly, out of interest, "What's your screenplay about?"

Imagining it's another hospital drama, or something along those lines, I'm surprised when he says with excitement, "A period drama. A romance set in the eighteen hundreds." He sighs. "It requires a lot of research on my part and that's why I need the privacy. I will have a researcher cast a look over each scene and make adjustments, but I must have some idea at least before I write it."

"It sounds amazing. I love that era." I'm not even joking because I am an avid fan of Downton Abbey and Bridgerton and can see why he chose that period.

"Then I'll run it past your critical eye for advice."

"Oh." I'm shocked and feel myself blush. "I'm not an expert or anything; my opinion wouldn't be worth much."

"Nonsense, you are the perfect person to give me your opinion because you're my target audience and your input will be invaluable."

He turns and says over his shoulder, "I think we'll work well together, Eliza. This should be fun."

As he leaves me surrounded by the most amazing scenery on the edge of paradise, I congratulate myself on making the best decision of my life. Annalise Turtle would be so proud of me, and I feel smug satisfaction that everything has slotted so well into place.

With a spring in my step, I turn and head back to the annexe to unpack and begin the adventure of a lifetime.

CHAPTER 4

*T*he annexe is comfortable, clean, and possibly the most luxurious accommodation I have ever inhabited. As I unpack my cases, I congratulate myself on a plan coming together and wonder what my co-workers in London would say if they could see me. In fact, just imagining what I would be doing now fills me with a sense of pride that I made this giant leap at all. It would have been so easy to stick with the familiar, the safe and the mundane, but now I have six months of contemplation to steer me in the right direction.

Thinking of Bill Monroe, I can't believe how lucky I am. He's a sweetheart. Kind, funny and gorgeous. The sort of man I would like to marry one day. His wife must count herself lucky, and I wonder why he felt the need to distance himself from his family. They could have come with him and enjoyed a break of the most relaxing kind. Then again, I wouldn't be here, so I'm happy for his reasons because it benefits me too.

Heading into the kitchen, I rummage around to familiarise myself with my new office. It all seems perfectly ok, if you're at home with all things domestic, but it's starting to dawn on me that I know nothing at all. Like Bill's son, I rely heavily on my mother to carry out that side of things and so this will be a steeper learning curve than I first thought. Mind you, how hard can it be?

Glancing at the modern range cooker, it fills me with horror because it looks like a beast. So many dials and diagrams on the front makes me wonder if I need a degree in engineering just to operate it.

Looking through the cupboards, I try to memorise where everything is and tentatively reach for a saucepan to see if boiling water is as easy as they say it is.

The tap is difficult to negotiate, and scalding hot water pours out, giving me a facial of the most extreme kind. Swallowing hard, I try to think back on those commercials I've seen for state-of-the-art kitchens and realise this is one of them. A boiling water tap that was all the rage a while ago. Even my mother insisted on having one for Christmas. Not that she got it course because my father prefers to live in the dark ages and would be content if we lit a fire in the garden and cooked on a cast-iron pot suspended over it.

My father is the king of the barbeque, and it's his answer to everything and God forbid anyone else offers to cook. The ferocious gleam in his eye followed by a terse, 'this is a man's job' brings out his inner caveman. The fact my mother runs around after him, bringing him cooling beers and prepping the marinade and salads, doesn't count when he announces she can 'take the night off and leave him to do the work.' The fact she works even harder catering to his demands causes quite a few arguments, especially when he announces with a satisfied sigh of relief that as he cooked, we can clean up. I'm just surprised he hasn't been skewered on his own barbeque by now.

The thought of family gatherings always makes me giggle because it causes so many arguments that are always the same. Nevertheless, it's a family tradition that will never die because as soon as the sun hits the patio in early April, he declares it barbeque season and we are resigned to the same procedure for the next six months.

As I make my third attempt to light the gas, I worry that I've got this job under false pretences. Maybe stating that cookery was my hobby, and I hoped to open a cake shop one day, was a step too far because water is seriously difficult to boil if you ask me.

After a fashion, I manage to get it bubbling away and look with pride at the first hurdle jumped with ease. I wonder what I should put in it?

What do people boil water for? I don't really know and so I turn to the pull-out larder cupboard and just wish I had one for my toiletries. It's so easy seeing everything laid out before you in rows, and I wonder if I can somehow persuade my father to install one of these in my wardrobe. Better still, he may even relent and convert the spare bedroom to a dressing room. I would absolutely love that.

Remembering Bill's comment about the shopping delivery, I wonder if I should head to the village and stock up on a few essentials to keep us going. We could certainly do with some Pringles, then there are the digestives Bill requires. I imagine it would be a necessity to purchase a bottle of wine and maybe some crudities and dips. Mum always puts those out when we have visitors. Cereal would be good; I wonder if they do sugar puffs here. I really fancy some chocolate as well. That would be a nice snack to feed my energy levels.

Maybe I should make a list of these essentials and see if I can borrow his car. Then again, I quite like the idea of cycling there. A rather fetching pastel coloured bike with a matching basket on the front would be good. I could fill it with fresh flowers from the local florists. That would certainly brighten up the place. Yes, I'm feeling quite domesticated already and as my water boils merrily away, I snap a quick photo and send it to my mum with the caption.

Domesticated goddess.

She must be holding her phone because her swift reply makes me smile.

Wow. Look at you! I'm so proud of my girl. Now, what do you propose to do with it?

She follows it with several laughing emojis, and I type back,

What do you suggest?

Pasta maybe, some rice perhaps.

My thoughts exactly. I'll let you know how it pans out (Crying with laughter emoji)

Almost immediately, she types back.

Tell me about Bill Monroe. Is he seriously gorgeous in real life? Has he proposed to you yet, or better still, asked for my number?

She doesn't even wait for my reply and types,

Send photos. Maybe when he's without a shirt. Send several. P.S. Don't let him catch you. He'll think you're a pervert.

My response is a gif of a woman rolling her eyes with the caption **FFS**

Tossing my phone to the side, I carefully turn off the pot of boiling water and consider lesson one done and dusted. It's all plain sailing from here and my thoughts turn to the cleaning side of things.

I'm pleased to note that the place is immaculate and probably only requires a flick of the occasional duster to keep it in shape. I imagine it will take around five minutes a day while I sing show tunes like Mary Poppins. I am really beginning to see the appeal of domestic life and count my lucky stars that a real star advertised for help. Yes, this is better than admin work in a local solicitors. Legal jargon that throws sand in my eyes and renders me stupefied.

This is my future; I just know it and so I tap out a shopping list on my phone and head off in search of my generous employer.

After trying several doors, I finally locate him at the top of the house in a room overlooking the calm, sparkling ocean. I knock tentatively, although the door is open, and he spins around at his desk that is set against the huge window and smiles.

"Eliza, have you settled in ok?"

"Yes, it's perfectly lovely."

I say shyly, "I was thinking of heading into the village for a few essentials. I don't suppose there's a bike handy I can use to get me there. I mean…" I hastily add, "I'm sure it's not far. I could probably walk if not."

"It's fine. I'll drive you. I quite fancy checking out the village myself."

"Oh, I don't want to interrupt your work."

He sighs. "There is no work as it happens."

"Excuse me?"

My first red flag waves violently in my face as his words sink in. No work, but…

"I just can't get the first sentence out. Writer's block before I've even begun. Maybe a break is just what I need to grab some inspiration from the village shop, along with the provisions."

He shuts down his computer and as I follow him outside, I'm feeling a little concerned that six months won't be long enough.

CHAPTER 5

*D*ream Valley town is much smaller than Whitstable and every bit as charming. Small white fronted shops sit atop little verandas with brightly filled flowerpots and the occasional string of bunting waving in the breeze. The small town is bustling with shoppers, although town is far too generous a word in my opinion. It looks like a dirty Disney. Pretty little buildings that could use the odd coat of paint here and there and a road sweeper to blast through the dusty street that runs the centre of it. It's almost like a throwback to the wild west, and I fall in love at first sight.

Bill parks his Cherokee Jeep in a nearby space and whistles with appreciation. "Civilisation at last, although it's a far cry from Wimbledon village. My wife would have a seizure."

He obviously finds this funny, and I say with interest, "Does she enjoy shopping, then?"

"Just a little."

He winks. "It's why I work. To keep my wife in the 'necessities', as she calls them. Necessary for her sanity more like it, although I indulge her passion out of necessity for my own."

"Your own?"

"It keeps Julia happy, which means I'm happy. It's the secret to a happy marriage. Keep the wife happy and she will be your best friend, among other things, of course."

He winks, leaving me feeling a little hot and bothered as I follow him out of the car.

We are parked outside a shop called Valley Marketplace, and I'm guessing we will find everything we need inside.

Bill strides forward, leaving me to bring up the rear and, like a true gentleman, he holds the door open for me and follows me inside.

This place is crammed full of everything we may need and as we grab a basket each, I whisper, "Do you want to choose, and I'll follow behind?"

"I wouldn't know what to buy. No, I'll follow your lead, Eliza. You know way more than I do about shopping for groceries."

Really wishing I hadn't made such a big thing of my glorious career in the local supermarket while I was at college, I smile with a confidence I don't feel. It's true, I did work Saturdays and the odd evening in our local superstore, but I was detailed with stocking the fashion shelves. I had zero contact with actual groceries and most of my shifts involved eyeing up the guys my age who stacked the shelves and gossiping with my friends who stopped by for a chat.

Now I smile with a confidence I don't feel inside and cast my 'expert' eye over the crates of fruit and veg.

"Um, Bill..."

"Yes, Eliza."

"Can you remember what was on order in your grocery delivery? I mean, maybe we should just grab a few necessities for today and take stock when it arrives."

"I don't know?" He shrugs, looking unconcerned. "Julia arranges all that and who knows what she ordered?"

Feeling a little relieved at that, I'm glad that she has taken charge and expect I'll see what type of things he likes when the delivery arrives. Feeling more confident, I say as if I know what I'm doing, "Then we'll just choose what we like until it arrives. Any preferences?"

"Not really. Just coffee, tea, and digestives, oh and maybe some bacon and eggs for a fry up in the morning." He leans in and whispers, "I'm not allowed that at home, so I intend on making the most of my freedom. I do love a good, cooked breakfast."

Deciding that the rising panic attack can be googled later, I nod and turn to the snack aisle. "Shall we get some Pringles?"

He follows me to familiar territory and starts tossing every flavour of Pringles they stock into the basket.

"Do we need all of these?"

My eyes are wide as he shrugs. "Probably. We may as well go for it, don't you think?"

I soon need a new basket because this one appears to be full already with snacks, crisps, peanuts, and every flavour of popcorn they stock. Turning to the next aisle, Bill fills his own basket with bottles of wine, beer, and a litre bottle of gin. Groaning under the weight of it, he places it on the floor and grabs another. This time he adds soft drinks, tonics and lemons and then looks around with a considered expression. "What have we missed?"

"Vitamins, minerals, and proteins, I'm guessing." I laugh as he winks cheekily in my direction. "I think we've covered the sugar content, not to mention the carbohydrates." Looking around, he spies the frozen section and grins. "Dairy next. What's your favourite ice cream flavour?"

"Chocolate – obviously." I roll my eyes as he laughs out loud. "Do you think they do pistachio?"

"Doubtful."

By now I've noticed a few curious glances in our direction, and I even see somebody filming us on their phone and feeling like Kevin Costner in The Bodyguard, I move in front of him and block him from view, whispering, "It appears you've been busted. If you like, I'll finish up here and you can retreat to the safety of the jeep."

He looks past me and grins, saying loudly, "It's fine. I'll even pose for photos if they like."

The sound of stampeding humans drowns out my reply and as I leave him surrounded by enthusiastic locals, I heave our baskets one by one towards the checkout area.

A smiling lady greets me, and I'm not surprised, judging by the amount of high-priced stuff we've bought, and she says pleasantly, "You must be the new occupants of Rock House. Rumour got here before you did, and we've all been dying to catch a glimpse of a bona fide celebrity."

Seeing Bill posing for selfies and laughing with the crowd makes me warm towards him even more.

"He's a great guy."

"Is he your father?"

The woman begins ringing up the items and I say quickly, "No, my boss."

Her arched brows say it all and she nods. "Of course."

I can tell she thinks this is a euphemism for something else and I blurt out, "I'm his housekeeper."

"If you say so, love."

She actually winks and I feel myself blushing as I say in a rather high-pitched voice, "No, really, I'm Eliza Benson. Mr Monroe hired me to take care of him."

Once again, she nods with a smirk on her face, and I feel my face heating as I dig myself into a very large hole.

Then I hear a gentle, "Hi, you must be Mr Monroe's housekeeper, he told me he was expecting you."

Looking around, I see a pretty woman staring at me with a welcoming smile, holding a basket of groceries as she listens in on our conversation with an amused look in her eye.

She grins. "I'm Sammy Jo Hudson. The agent who rented

Rock House to Mr Monroe. I met him yesterday when he arrived, and he told me he was expecting you."

My heart sags with relief because she isn't judging me at all, unlike the disbelieving shop keeper who is probably imagining all sorts.

Sammy Jo looks like an angel, and she obviously deserves the job title because she says sweetly, "I'll give you my number in case you need any information. It can be quite lonely here when you don't know anyone, and Mr Monroe asked me to look out for you."

"He did?"

I flick a look at the man himself and he grins from across the room as our eyes meet.

"He's a sweetheart." Sammy Jo voices my own thoughts and she says to the woman ringing up the national debt, "Do you recognise him, Mrs Bevan?"

"Of course. I've been ticking the days off my calendar since I heard he was coming. It's about time something good happened around here."

I watch with interest as she plucks her phone from under the counter and takes a sneaky photo of Bill and I look at Sammy Jo and raise my eyes.

She grins at me, and I thank God for Sammy Jo Hudson. She looks around my own age and lots of fun. "Do you live in Dream Valley?"

I really hope she does, and she nods. "Yes, I moved here when I married my husband."

"That's nice. It seems a great place to live."

"£86.50 please." A loud voice interrupts our conversation and I turn and say with surprise, "As much as that?" I stare at Mrs Bevan in shock, and she nods, pointing to the gin and wine. "Alcohol adds up."

Bill shouts from across the room, "Take my card, Eliza." He holds up his credit card and I rush over, feeling self-conscious as just about every person in the shop looks at me in awe and points their phone cameras in my direction.

Grabbing it, I see his eyes twinkle mischievously and I can't help but giggle as I hurry back to pay.

"He looks like a lot of fun, Eliza."

Sammy smiles and I nod. "I think you're right. Lucky me."

As Mrs Bevan takes payment, Sammy Jo leans in and says softly, "Call me and we can meet up for a coffee. Don't be a stranger. This town is amazing and there are lots of great people here. I'm guessing life could get a little lonely at Rock House when Mr Monroe starts work, so call me. We can meet up and I'll fill you in on everything Dream Valley."

"Do you mind?" I'm relieved to find a friend at least, and she nods. "Of course, ask me anything."

Spying the bacon and eggs in the nearby carrier bag, I whisper, "I don't suppose you know how to cook; it's just I could really use some help in that department."

She looks past me to Bill and grins. "Interesting. This sounds like a story I need to hear. Leave it with me. I have the perfect teacher in mind."

As Mrs Bevan hands me Bill's card, she calls out, "Gerry, help the customer out to the car, will you?"

Looking up, I see a man gazing at me with what can only be described as awe, and I feel like a celebrity myself, as he sprints forward and grabs the bags effortlessly, while staring at me the whole time.

By now Bill has satisfied the curious locals and he reaches my side and grins at Sammy Jo. "Hey, we meet again."

"Mr Monroe." She nods, and he waves his hand, "Call me Bill." He turns his blinding smile to the shopkeeper and flashes her a smouldering look, that causes the heat to rush to her cheeks and her eyes to dilate. "And who is this lovely lady?"

He extends his hand, and she grasps it so quickly I wouldn't be surprised to see steam coming off it and holds on tight as she giggles, "Alice Bevan, shop proprietor, and font of all knowledge in Dream Valley."

"I'm pleased to meet you, Alice."

She flushes with pleasure and as Sammy Jo nudges me, I struggle to stop laughing.

"You have an amazing shop, Alice. I can see I'll be spending many happy hours in here."

He pulls away from the now speechless shop keeper and, turning to me, winks. "Ready, Eliza?"

I nod and as we follow Gerry to the car, I feel the curious stares follow us and wonder if this kind of attention is what Bill lives with every day of his life.

CHAPTER 6

*W*e place the bags in the car, and Bill looks around with satisfaction. "I think I'm going to like it here."

"It seems nice." I have to agree, and he points to a restaurant a few doors away. "Do you fancy grabbing an early meal in there? It looks good, and I'm sure you must be hungry by now."

I look where he's pointing and see the name, The Olive Tree, written in bold lettering above a painted door and note the fairy lights winding around the wooden frame of the veranda and the potted olive trees on either side of the door.

"I love Italian food." I say with happiness, and he nods in agreement. "Me too, although Julia limits me to one pasta dish a week to keep me 'balanced', as she calls it."

He grins impishly, "But she's not here now and I intend on making the most of my freedom. So, follow me, Eliza. I hope you're ready for a feast."

Once again, I feel that I made the best decision of my life as I follow him up the wooden steps towards the door of the Italian restaurant. My guardian angel is obviously doing a really good job of steering me in the right direction because Bill Monroe has been sent to me from the heavens.

We step inside and an attractive woman looks up and smiles, her eyes loaded with curiosity as Bill turns on the charm. "Hey, I don't suppose you have room for two strangers in town looking for a place to call their local for the next six months."

"Of course, sir, table for two?" She smiles and, like everyone else, it seems she can't do enough for him already. I'm not sure it's because he's famous either. Bill is just a really nice, friendly guy who knows how to turn on the charm and get people on his side.

She directs us to a table for two by the window and hands us some menus.

"Sally will take your order; she won't be long. Can I fetch you some drinks in the meantime?"

"A bottle of your finest red please and whatever Eliza wants, if it's different to that."

"Wine is fine." I say hastily because a whole bottle of wine between us will make for a very merry evening ahead if I'm not careful.

As we settle into our seats, I look at the charming interior of a very cosy restaurant. "I love Italian food." I repeat with enthusiasm, and Bill remarks, "Have you ever been to Italy?"

"Sadly, no. Have you?"

"Several times. It's an amazing place. You should go there."

"I should do a lot of things, which is why I broke ties with my old life and answered your ad."

He studies me with a thoughtful look. "So, tell me all about Eliza Benson."

"There's not much to tell outside my CV."

He shakes his head and leans forward, fixing me with his twinkling blue eyes, giving me nowhere to hide.

"Tell me why you applied for the job and not in an interview type of way; newsflash, you've got the job."

He grins, which makes me laugh because it's impossible not to around him and I sink back in my chair and sigh.

"I suppose I've reached that part in my life where I question everything. My past decisions. Were they really the right ones for me and what about my future? I still live at home. Apparently, it's all the rage these days." He laughs and nods in agreement. "I have one of my own at home so I can't argue with you there."

We are interrupted by the waitress returning with our drinks and she smiles. "Hi, I'm Maria and this is my restaurant. We pride ourselves on our service, and the food, of course."

She fixes us both with a friendly smile. "Let us know if we can improve on anything. There's always room for that."

"You're not wrong there, Maria." Bill replies and raises his wine glass to his lips and takes a practised swig before setting the glass down and nodding with appreciation. "Perfect already. The only way is down."

Maria laughs and says quickly, "I sincerely hope you're referring to the drink and not my establishment. Well, as I said, Sally will serve you and let me know what you think at the end of your meal."

She heads off and as I watch Bill pour some wine into my glass, I sigh with pleasure. "This is nice."

"It is." He looks up with a quizzical expression. "Anyway, you were saying…"

As I accept the glass of wine, I am forced to carry on with my potted history. "I wasn't sure if I wanted to be the woman in my office who has worked there for thirty years, and it took the last will and testament of one of our clients to convince me to take a chance. On that same day, I saw your advert and took it as a sign to go for it. Reckless, don't you think?"

"Sensible."

"Really?"

I laugh as I take another swig of my wine and Bill says with a grin, "You get nowhere in life if you're risk averse. My parents wanted me to be an accountant because that was all they knew. It pays well and I would have a comfortable life, but the thought of it bored me senseless. They tried every trick in the book to talk me out of acting, but I persevered by working in bars and selling shoes on Saturday to pay my way through drama school. I promised them that if I hadn't got a break in the first three years, I would go back to college and do what they wanted."

"That was brave."

"Not really. I made it my goal not to fail."

"So, what did you do?"

I am fascinated by his story, and he swirls the wine around his glass and looks at me steadily. "I auditioned for every part I saw. I researched the companies, the directors, and the plays them-selves. I struck up conversations with the staff at every event and I made sure to stand out from the crowd. You could say I worked the room, and it paid off because I landed a part on a low budget film and the rest is history."

"What did your parents say?"

"At first, they thought I was wasting my time. They were proud of me, don't get me wrong, but they were not the kind of people who took chances. Then, when I became more successful and earned more in a year than my father had in his lifetime, they conceded defeat."

He smiles sadly. "I had the chance to make my dream happen and now you have yours. The question is, what *is* your dream, Eliza?"

His question catches me off guard and I stare into my wine for the longest minute and then I say slightly wistfully, "I want to live, Bill. To look back when I'm old at a life that counted for something. I want to see the world and experience different cultures. I'm not saying I want to be rich, although I wouldn't say no if it happened."

He raises his glass to mine. "It does help with the other stuff."

"I'm sure." I think about what I want and I'm not sure if I can really answer him, but say wistfully, "Staying in the same job, with the same people, in the same town, feels like wasting my life.

I'm not saying that's wrong, but there's so much more out there. The case I was working on showed me another way. The lady who died was a career gold digger. She married men for their money and amassed a huge fortune. When she had it, she entertained young men with the same idea. I suppose you could say she was giving something back to society."

We grin through the candlelight, and I shrug. "That was her way, and it worked for her. She travelled, saw many amazing things and did it in style. I want to see where life takes me and not have a grand master plan to follow. My mother thinks I'm reckless, having some kind of crisis and stepping outside my lane in life, but if I do nothing else, I wanted to break free from my comfort zone and see what's on the other side."

He raises his glass to mine. "To new beginnings and new horizons for both of us."

As we clink glasses, it feels as if I've made a valuable friend in Bill Monroe. Two kindred spirits who are meeting by chance, on a road to nowhere, or to the most fantastic future. I'm in good company because Bill has been on this road before, and it gave him a great life. Now it's my turn and I am not going to waste a minute of it.

CHAPTER 7

I am such a fool. The cold light of day reminds me of that because after probably the most pleasant evening of my life, I stayed up way too late and not just because it took us over an hour to make the fifteen-minute journey home. Due to the fact we consumed two bottles of wine between us, we had to call a taxi and the one that arrived was the slowest one in the history of motoring. I doubt he got out of second gear and even stopped to check on his cows in a field in the middle of nowhere. Then, when we finally got on our way, he pulled over and starting shooting with an air rifle at a fox who crossed our path.

Bill thought the whole experience was hysterical and so did I, but for a very different reason. I have never worn hysteria well and fearing for my life, while being held hostage by a man with a loaded gun, didn't fill me with hope for any kind of future at all.

So much for my new bright new beginning. I started to doubt I had one and was so grateful when we rolled up at Rock House way past my bedtime.

Then I tried to make us coffee, and it turns out that's an art form too because Bill likes a cappuccino and how was I supposed to know how the machine works? In the end, we settled for two cups of tea, which left me loaded with anxiety because his parting shot before he staggered to bed was how much he was looking forward to his full English in the morning.

That put paid to any sleep for me, and I spent the whole night panicking about it and so it's now six am and I hope to God my mum is up already because this is an emergency.

Dashing off a quick text, I pray that she answers immediately.

Mum, are you up?

There's nothing but a blank screen and it doesn't even say she's online. In fact, she was last online at ten pm yesterday.

Hoping she rouses before Bill does, I plod into the kitchen and look around in dismay. There is bacon, eggs and bread, courtesy of Valley Marketplace and surely it can't be too difficult to cook them.

Rummaging around in the cupboards, I pull out a frying pan and wonder what I do next.

Grabbing my phone, I google it and as I watch a tutorial, I feel my resolve hardening. I can do this; it will be fine. Just toss them in the pan and hope for the best. Perfect.

By the time Bill surfaces, looking a little worse for wear, I am dressed and ready to face my first challenge.

"Morning, Eliza, how did you sleep?"

"Perfect, thank you."

I hope he can't see through my lies and luckily, he just nods. "I'm glad one of us did. You know, it was so quiet I could hear my own heart beating. It really freaked me out."

He runs his fingers through his hair and groans. "I regretted drinking that wine because I thought my time was up and my heart was going to punish me for putting it to work so hard. Maybe we should skip the fry up this morning and just eat fruit or something until my heart forgives me."

Thank. You. God.

I offer a silent prayer to the man who always knows how to

deliver and smile. "Maybe tomorrow then. Let me see what we have."

However, as I open the fridge, it's pretty obvious all we have is milk and, in the absence of the food delivery, a cupboard full of food that any heart would weep at.

"I don't think your heart will forgive you if you substitute fruit for Pringles and nuts. What are we going to do?"

Bill groans. "I forgot about that. Oh well, we'll just head back to town to pick up the car and grab some breakfast in the café we saw yesterday."

"If we make it there by lunchtime. Did you think that taxi was weird last night? I'm sure we could have walked faster."

"I forgot about that." Bill shakes his head. "I'll check what time the food delivery is and hopefully he'll be able to drop me off in town afterwards."

"Do you think he would?"

I'm surprised at that, but Bill just nods. "I'll pay him. That always works."

"I suppose so."

Bill heads off, leaving me feeling like a failure already. Some housekeeper I am. I can't make anything except boiled water, it seems, and Bill has angered his heart already under my watch. Thinking of my encounter with Sammy Jo yesterday, I decide to call her at the first chance I get to arrange those lessons because as Bill said last night, if I'm to achieve anything in life, it's to study hard and set my goal and mine is to become the best housekeeper he has ever employed, or die trying.

* * *

OUR FIRST BREAK comes when Bill announces the shopping is due in one hour, so we make do with yet more tea and some digestives and wait for the miracle of online shopping to arrive.

By the time the shopping is offloaded, and Bill is firmly beside

41

the driver heading into Dream Valley, I am left to organise the food that was ordered by his loving wife. I say loving because it appears she definitely wants his heart to love her because everything is half fat, zero fat, probiotic, lactose free and gluten-free. This food delivery could win awards for nutrition, and I have never seen anything more boring in my life. This is a disaster. There isn't even a chocolate digestive in sight, and where is the full cream milk? The stuff she ordered is milk residue in my opinion and doesn't deserve the title.

Thinking back on the cows we passed, I wonder if they do a takeaway milk order because I absolutely cannot exist on milk residue for even one cup of tea, let alone six months.

Finally, my mum calls and I snatch the phone eagerly.

"Hi, mum, about time too."

"What do you mean?"

"I needed your advice."

"Already, why?"

"He wanted a full English."

Her laughter reaches me before any advice and I snap, "It's fine. His heart wasn't feeling it today, so we had a digestive instead."

"That poor man. I feel his pain."

"Why? What's wrong with your heart? Shall I come home?"

She sighs down the phone. *"Get a grip, Eliza, you're panicking. Take a few deep breaths and exhale slowly."*

I do as she says, and she murmurs, *"Better?"*

"Thanks, mum."

I sigh down the phone. "I'm going to be fired, aren't I?"

"Only if you approach it with that attitude, young lady. No, this could be your finest hour, darling. Now, take stock, take one step at a time, and hold your nerve and repeat after me. I'm a domesticated goddess and nothing will beat me."

"I'm a domesticated goddess and nothing will beat me."

"Good. Now, tell me what's wrong."

I fill her in on events so far and she says in a practical voice, *"First thing is to call that number and request help from the good Samaritan you met yesterday. Take a few lessons and move one step at a time. If you must, buy a few ready meals and wing it. Then, when you get more confident, you can unleash your inner creative and wow him with your excellence."*

Despite how serious the situation is, I laugh. 'Thanks, mum. I'll call the number.'

"So, what's he like? Is he seriously gorgeous?"

"Yes, he is."

"Are you allowed visitors yet?"

"No, mum. Definitely no visitors."

"When then?"

"No visitors – period."

"What, for six months? Of course you can see your family in that time. Shall we pencil something in? Next week is good for me."

"Mum…" I feel the pressure mounting. "Please, one thing at a time. I need to focus on keeping this job, not adding to the list of reasons to fire me."

"Ok, if you insist. Right then, he's out, you say, and is probably already eating breakfast in a place that knows how to prepare them, so you've dodged that bullet at least. My advice would be to call the number, get some lessons and, in the meantime, google a recipe with the ingredients you've got. I'm sure you can follow instructions, so it won't be difficult. You're an intelligent woman and I have faith you can do this. You know, I blame myself. This should have been addressed years ago. Your father always said I did too much for you and this is the result. Maybe it was a good thing you took this job. It could be the making of you and…"

"Sorry mum, there's someone at the door, love you."

I cut the call because once my mother gets on the subject of how useless I am, there will be no stopping her and I don't need a reminder of that at the moment because it's perfectly obvious that she's right and I need help, in every aspect of my life.

As I organise the cupboards and look at what I'm working with, I decide to follow her advice and call the number.

Luckily, Sammy Jo answers on the first ring and just hearing her calm, in control voice chases any nerves away.

"Oh Hi, Sammy Jo, it's Eliza Benson. We met yesterday in the store in town."

"Oh yes, how's it going?"

"Well, I could use some help. I hope you don't mind?"

"Of course not. How can I help?"

"Those cookery lessons you mentioned. I don't suppose they're available sometime today."

She doesn't even hesitate and says, "Leave it with me, Eliza. I'll arrange it and we'll be there within the hour."

I breathe a sigh of relief. "Really, thank goodness, you're a life saver."

I'm definitely thinking of Bill's heart here because if he gives out on me, it will be all my fault and so as I cut the call, I count to ten and hope to God the person she sends is a miracle worker.

CHAPTER 8

$\mathcal{B}$ ill returned, and as mum said, he stopped by a place called the Cosy Kettle for breakfast. He was so apologetic and yet I couldn't be happier. At least he's been fed already and as he heads off to his office to start his screenplay, I'm left to learn everything I should already know, on a crash course of the most desperate kind.

Exactly one hour later, I hear a car pull up and quickly rush to meet my visitors before they can disturb Bill and I see Sammy Jo and a woman who is older than us, looking at me with curiosity.

"Thank you so much for coming." I usher them inside and as I close the kitchen door, I exhale a huge sigh of relief.

"This is so good of you."

Sammy Jo nods towards her companion. "Allow me to introduce Mrs Jenkins. She's a whizz with all things domestic and will be the best teacher."

Mrs Jenkins smiles. "I would be happy to help. What do you need to know?"

"Um everything." I smile guiltily, and Sammy Jo looks amused. "You will definitely tell me this story later, but for now I'll leave you in Mrs Jenkins' capable hands and come back in a couple of hours. Is that ok, Mrs Jenkins?"

"Of course, love, leave this with me."

As I walk Sammy Jo out, I whisper, "You're a lifesaver. I can't thank you enough."

"It's my pleasure. Anyway, why don't we meet later for a drink? I could come and pick you up if you like."

"I'll have to check with Bill first, if that's ok. I'm so new I don't know what's expected of me time wise but if he says it's ok, of course I'd love to meet you."

"That's fine. Just text me when you can."

She smiles and heads off in her car, leaving me feeling so grateful I met her. As I head inside, I find Mrs Jenkins peering in the fridge and looking thoughtful.

"What do you think?" I look at her anxiously.

"It's fine. I'm guessing you need something for lunch and then dinner, and possibly a few healthy snacks to graze on during the day."

"All of the above." I sigh with relief. "Anyone would think you were an expert."

She laughs and I love how her eyes twinkle. "I've been doing this long enough."

"Doing what?"

"A housekeeper. I've worked for the Hudsons for more years than I care to admit, and they have asked for most things, so I think I've got you covered."

"Sammy Jo's family?"

She nods. "Yes, Sammy Jo's husband lives with his mother and three brothers at Valley House. I've been working there since before they were born and a nicer family you would struggle to meet."

"Well, Sammy Jo is certainly the nicest person I've met in a long time."

Mrs Jenkins' expression softens. "She's an angel, and she needs to be with Marcus as her husband."

She laughs, but I see the fondness in her eyes as she talks about him. "He's a handful but is a different person with her. They say it takes a strong woman to deal with a strong man and they got that right. For all her soft edges, she's hard where it counts, and they make the perfect team. Anyway..." she looks around. "We don't have long, so let's make a start."

For the next hour, Mrs Jenkins gives me a crash course in cookery. Somehow, she rustles up an easy lunch of salad with grilled chicken and even a delicious homemade dressing for the leaves. In fact, she uses ingredients I would never have imagined belonged in a salad and the results are amazing but simple. Then she prepares an evening meal of beef casserole, that she assures me will slow cook in the range for most of the day. I help her peel vegetables and watch with interest as she demonstrates how to construct a meal. She even has time to make some granola bars from scratch and a lemon drizzle cake that is made with half fat ingredients. The smells in the kitchen are divine and I am feeling extremely satisfied with my ingenious plan to get a professional in.

By the time Sammy Jo returns, the kitchen smells like heaven and we have made a pot of coffee and arranged a tray to take up to Bill for elevenses.

Sammy Jo looks impressed, and I even think I've learned something. I have my notes on my phone with a detailed to do list consisting of timings and instructions and I think I have survived the first day of meals at least.

Mrs Jenkins promises to return tomorrow after she has finished at the Hudson's and has agreed to give me a crash course in domestic bliss, lasting a week.

"I don't know how I can repay you for this."

I feel like hugging the domestic goddess as she leaves, and she says warmly, "Just seeing you learn will be payment enough. You know, if you have any questions, just call, or text me."

I'm so grateful she gave me her number and I think I can do anything with the back-up I now have.

As I wave them off, I feel happy about how things are going. Day one and I think I've got this. I may even be able to explore the beach later. I am itching to do that and as I head inside Rock House, I'm feeling quite good about life.

* * *

I FINALLY MAKE it to the beach after lunch. Bill seems happy. His writer's block has shifted, and he has started writing the first scene. He was more than happy with lunch and told me to take some time this afternoon to explore. So, the first place on my list was the beach and now I'm out in the fresh air, I am thinking more clearly.

Dreamy Sand Beach is a magical place. Fine sand that frames a sparkling ocean, where the waves gently roll to shore, courtesy of the land that juts out to sea either side of it. A natural wind break that provides shelter. It's quiet too, save for a couple of people walking their dogs. I'm sure it will get busier the warmer the weather gets, but for now it feels like my own private haven from the world. It feels good as the breeze blows the cobwebs away, making me feel better about my rash decision to quit my job for the unknown.

Luckily, I brought my book with me, and I decide to sit with my back against a rock and read for a while. The sun kisses the top of my head and I feel the warmth spread through my limbs as I escape inside the pages. In fact, this life is idyllic and just imagining the workers in London, beavering away in their offices, and grabbing a quick sushi at lunchtime, strikes horror in my heart. I was right to escape for my mental health because there is nothing that compares to the way I'm feeling now.

The seagulls call overhead, and the gentle lapping of the waves are my companions, as I absorb myself in a dystopian tale about the end of the world — perfect.

* * *

BY THE TIME I return to Rock House, I am re-energised and ready to tackle anything, and I even manage to boil the kettle and make the tea. Arranging the tray with a slice of Mrs Jenkins' lemon drizzle and a mug of freshly brewed tea, I feel as if I'm living my best life.

"Hi, Eliza, you're a sight for sore eyes."

Bill smiles as I enter the room, balancing the tray as I negotiate the door.

"I thought you may need sustenance."

He spies the cake and his eyes light up. "I thought I detected the aroma of baking. I must say, this is a treat I don't normally enjoy. I'm lucky if I get a rice cake with my herbal tea."

He groans and seizes the tray eagerly and I feel a little concerned that I'm missing something here.

"You can eat cake, can't you? I mean…" I hastily add, "You're not allergic to sugar or anything like that."

He laughs out loud. "No, the only thing I'm allergic to is people telling me what to do."

Shaking his head, he sighs. "Julia means well, but I had to escape for my continued sanity. She belongs to so many women's groups I can't keep up and it appears all they talk about is how to make their husband's lives miserable."

This is awkward, and I shift nervously on my feet as he laughs. "It's all about wellness now, apparently. Your body is your temple and God forbid you ask for sugar in your tea. Not that you get normal tea anymore. It's all peppermint, ginger, and that green stuff these days, which tastes like swamp water. Apparently, that's good for you."

Rolling his eyes, he takes a large bite of lemon drizzle and groans, winking mischievously in appreciation.

"This tastes so good." He looks out of the window and sighs. "Look at that, Eliza. That view does more for my wellness than any rank smoothie or alfalfa bean salad. A nice piece of cake and calm perfection is worth more than any health regime. I feel energised, rested, and happy, which is more than I can say when I'm strapped to a heart monitor, doing five miles in the gym on the running machine. A gentle stroll along the beach is worth more than a power walk around Wimbledon common, while attempting to reach my step count for the day. Wouldn't you agree?"

"Wholeheartedly." I feel sympathetic towards Bill because it sounds as if his wife means well but is rather over eager and I guess that's because of the people she mixes with and the life they lead.

Bill finishes the cake in a contemplative silence and so I say nervously, "I should leave you in peace."

"It's fine." He raises his eyes and smiles. "I love my own company, but it's also good to talk to someone other than myself. So, how was your morning? I must say that lunch was fabulous and even Julia would struggle to criticise the nutritional value, and it didn't taste like twigs off the forest floor."

"I'm glad you liked it."

I wonder if I should come clean because it seems wrong taking credit for someone else's work and yet it feels good to be praised for something for once. Nobody ever praises me. Even Mr Henderson, who was always finding fault with my work but always relied on me to take on the more complicated tasks. I know I'm good at what I do, but that's where it ends. I'm not good at life, as it turns out, which is why this is so good for me.

Bill exhales and says with regret, "I should get back to it. I have the next scene in my head, and I need to get it down."

"Of course, just yell if you need anything."

Gathering the tray and the empty mug and plate, I head back to my domain and make a decision. I will embrace this new life and become the best assistant, slash housekeeper, he has ever had and who knows, I may even make a career of it. I will form my own domesticated bliss company where I will recruit and provide people like me to families all over the world. It will be global; an international business that takes the world by storm. I will attend conferences and become a public speaker, telling the world how domestic bliss has built a multi-million-dollar brand. Yes, that will be my life. I will be invincible but first I need to work out how to use the hoover.

CHAPTER 9

A few days later and I'm feeling a lot better about things. Mrs Jenkins arrives at eleven each morning and gives me a masterclass in all things domestic. Sammy Jo drops her off most days, and we have agreed to meet up on Friday night, when she will pick me up at seven and take me to a place called The Toasty Tipple in a town called Riverton.

It will be my first proper evening out and I'm excited about it.

Bill seems happy, and I'm guessing it's because Mrs Jenkins is a culinary genius. She has prepared so many amazing meals from the frankly, shocking ingredients that Julia ordered, but somehow, she makes them taste fantastic. Even the Pringles have remained un-popped because the various cakes and biscuits she's prepared, not to mention the freshly baked bread she demonstrated how to make yesterday, are far more enjoyable snacks than any manufactured ones. Coupled with the sea air and sunshine, I'm feeling so much better than I did when I arrived.

Bill looks rested and happy, and we have got into the habit of taking an afternoon stroll on the beach, where we discuss the universe and make the world a better place.

Bill's friendship is the most surprising thing about this job. He is seriously amazing. Kind, funny and clever. His stories are engrossing and his wit sharp, making me laugh until the tears roll down my cheeks. Yes, Bill Monroe is the full package, and I can see why so many women have fallen heavily for this man who is perfect in every way.

* * *

FRIDAY NIGHT COMES and I am nervous but excited about my first night out. Bill is staying in to watch Netflix with a bowl of popcorn and is looking forward to a night of indulgence, which he assures me is the best treat possible because he can't remember the last time he was allowed.

Sammy Jo picks me up at seven in a smart Range Rover and, as we head off, she says with interest, "So, how was your first week?"

"A lot better for Mrs Jenkins."

She nods, "She's amazing, isn't she?"

"I couldn't have coped without her help."

"So, tell me, Eliza, how does someone who can't boil an egg land a job as a housekeeper to one of the most sought-after celebrities on our daytime screens? Please fill me in. I'm dying with curiosity."

Grinning like an idiot, I laugh. "Fate, I suppose. I was working in a solicitor's office in London and saw my life following the same pattern for the next thirty years. Then I read about an impressive woman who did some amazing things. It made me look at my own life and then I saw the advert for this job. I suppose I wouldn't have applied if I hadn't been feeling restless and I never really thought about what was involved, just the idea."

Sammy laughs softly. "You sound like me and my friend Florrie. Sometimes it takes one thing to spark a reaction that changes everything. A systemic shift in the atmosphere and I know a lot about that."

"How?"

"Florrie was getting married, and it turned out her groom was already married, a fact that only came to light as she walked down the aisle at her own wedding."

"That's terrible." I'm shocked and she giggles. "Well, we went on their honeymoon instead and met the Hudson brothers. Strange things happened, and we came here to start a new life with them."

"That's… astonishing."

"You don't know the half of it. It's definitely been an interesting experience, and I know a lot about wanting change. I've been there and now I'm wearing the t-shirt. I think it's the right move, though. Whatever your reasons, they were meant to lead you here and now it will be interesting to see where you end up."

"I'm not sure. Part of me is dreading the end of this because what will happen then? Bill will return home and I'll be looking for the next adventure."

"I understand the rental is for six months. You have time on your side, at least."

"Yes." I smile happily. "Six months to figure everything out."

Sammy turns on the indicator and I look with interest at the cosy looking pub that looms up before us. It sits on the side of a busy road, and we pull into a space in the car park. As she cuts the engine, she sighs. "Here at last. You know, this place is a godsend because even though it's a short drive, it gets you out of Dream Valley and into civilisation, which is necessary sometimes."

We head off down the path and I say with interest, "Dream Valley seems a great place to live."

"It is. More than amazing. It's just so full on most of the time and occasionally it's good to get away."

We head into the pub, and it's strange seeing other people

because it's just been Bill, Mrs Jenkins, and me for a week already.

Sammy points to a table by the window.

"Grab that and I'll fetch the drinks. What would you like?"

"Just a white wine, please."

I reach for my purse, and she shakes her head. "It's fine, my treat. You can get the next one."

As I take my seat, I look around with interest. The Toasty Tipple is just perfect. Old world charm courtesy of beams with brasses nailed to them. Rustic wooden furniture that's mismatched and appears to have been collected from old house clearances. A roaring inglenook fireplace that is currently empty due to the pre-summer balmier nights. The oak bar is polished until it gleams and is set along one wall where the patrons stand and lean against it as they laugh with their friends. It's a comfortable place to come and socialise and it feels good to enjoy an evening of good conversation in a warm and welcome environment.

As the evening progresses, I am brought up to speed on life in Dream Valley. Sammy Jo fills me in on how it works, who's who, and makes me laugh with stories about her family and what they get up to. It all sounds idyllic and just seeing the happiness in her eyes tells me she found her happily ever after here with the interesting sounding Marcus Hudson.

I wonder if my own life will work out so well.

CHAPTER 10

$\mathcal{T}$he next couple of weeks follow much the same pattern. Mrs Jenkins stops by to help educate me, and Bill reaps the rewards. Sammy Jo helps with my social life, and we have enjoyed coffee and chats and some walks where she introduced me to the local area. Dream Valley appears to be the perfect place to live. Modern life is there if you want it, but not a necessity.

Bill has been the perfect employer, and we have grown a friendship that I value above everything else.

So, I'm alarmed when I take him his morning coffee with a slice of Mrs Jenkins' fruit cake and see him looking worried.

"Is everything ok?" I set the tray down on his desk and wonder if the screenplay has stagnated again.

"Sorry, Eliza, I tried to stop them."

"Stop who?"

I'm not even sure of who *they* are, and he groans.

"Julia insists on visiting this weekend with Blake. She told me she wasn't taking no for an answer, and she needed to check up on me."

"I suppose that's natural."

of the stairs. "I'll come with you if you like. I should get my hair cut."

"Really."

I look at him in surprise and he nods as he takes two steps at a time. "Julia won't appreciate anything but excellence. If I'm to convince her that everything is fine and we're coping I need to tidy up."

He looks a little anxious, "What about the crisps etc? Can you hide them somewhere?"

"Of course, I'll pack them in my suitcase."

"Good." He looks as if his mind's racing and is mentally checking off boxes in his head. "Let's make sure we have lots of the fresh stuff in the fridge. You can stow the gin in the garage. She wouldn't be seen dead in there."

"Garage, of course."

He rubs his chin in thought. "Flowers. We need lots of them and air freshener."

"My thoughts exactly."

Looking around, his eagle eyes miss nothing. "We need to hoover, mop the floors and make sure there are no streaks on the windows."

Goodness, this woman must be a monster. I can't believe he is taking this so seriously and now I'm even more nervous than before.

"Maybe we should get you a uniform?"

"You're not serious."

He looks apologetic. "Sorry, she would approve of that, but if you like, just wear an apron or something and tie back your hair. Julia is a stickler for hygiene and our own housekeeper in Wimbledon is forced to always wear a hairnet."

"You have a housekeeper?" Now I'm feeling even more inferior, and he nods. "Only twice a week. She comes in and cleans, organises, and prepares snacks to last the week. She's a saint and for some reason she idolises Julia, which is a good thing because she is housekeeper number fifteen and counting."

"I need to sit down." I flop onto the bench by the front door and Bill looks concerned. "It's fine, *she's* fine. I shouldn't have said anything, really. Just be yourself, Eliza, and don't take anything personally."

He grabs the keys from the pot by the door and says quickly, "Come on, we need all the time we can get."

* * *

ONCE AGAIN, we park opposite Valley Marketplace and while I head inside to stock up on healthy options and possibly a few bunches of flowers, Bill heads off to the hair salon across the street to see if they can fit him in at short notice. As I start stuffing baskets, Mrs Bevan shouts, "Good to see you, Eliza. How are things at Rock House?"

"Complicated, Mrs Bevan, and getting more complicated by the hour."

"Really?" I hear the interest surge across the shop floor and say loudly, "Visitors. We need more supplies."

"Oh, I see. Anyone famous?"

"No. Bill's family."

"Oh." She sounds disappointed about that. "I thought we'd see a few celebrity parties. You know, the kind of shenanigans that make it to the news. I'm preparing for the press onslaught to stake out the area and I'm really hoping that lovely Eamonn Holmes comes to stay."

"I'm sorry." I have half an ear on her conversation and the other half of me is in panic mode as I try to think about what I'm buying.

"Yes, I love a bit of Eamonn. It's that lilting Irish accent that makes me weak at the knees. Imagine living with a man like that. Gerry!"

I jump and almost drop the probiotic yoghurt drink I'm balancing on top of a low-fat tub of Greek yoghurt. "Come and help Eliza to the car."

Loud footsteps come running and Mrs Bevan whisper shouts, "I think he's sweet on you, dear. I've just made his day."

As Gerry bursts out from the back of the shop in his red lumberjack shirt and ginger afro, I shiver a little. The lecherous way he openly stares at me makes my skin crawl, and yet I maintain a polite smile and continue stuffing items into the growing pile of baskets at speed.

Soon, I've amassed enough food for a month and as Mrs Bevan rings it up, I try desperately not to engage Gerry in conversation and pretend to be engrossed in the notes section of my phone.

Luckily, Bill heads in and says, out of breath, "Sorted."

I look up and see his sharp haircut and he grins. "No problem. There was a lovely lady in there called Jemima. She was about to go on her lunch break but made an exception for me."

"I bet she did." Mrs Bevan cuts in and Bill turns to her and lays on the charm with the proverbial trowel.

"Ah, Alice, my lovely friend who supplies everything I need."

Her cheeks blush and her eyes turn glassy, and I can only imagine what thoughts are running through her head right now.

It's strange watching an overbearing woman crumble with just a few words and makes for a moment of enjoyment. She reverts to a tongue-tied schoolgirl as she giggles and blushes, while looking at him coyly with her eyelashes fluttering. I just stare in wonder as he leans closer and whispers something in her ear, which makes her giggle, and as he turns, he winks at me before straightening up and reaching for his wallet. "How much do I owe you, lovely lady?"

"Well, as it you..." she winks suggestively. "I'll offer you a special five per cent discount. I only offer that to family and friends, you know, so consider yourself one of us now."

"I'm flattered." He flashes her a blinding smile and hands over his credit card and as she finalises the transaction, Gerry appears at my side and whispers, "Where shall I stick this?" Bill snorts as I jump in surprise and register the bag Gerry is holding in his hands and say quickly, "Bill will show you."

Leaning down and grabbing an armful of grocery bags, we say our goodbyes and head back to the jeep.

Leaving Bill to deal with Gerry, I spy a lovely little gift shop a few doors along and say quickly, "I'll just go and see if they have a scented candle or air freshener in there. I won't be long."

"Good idea, get what you need." Bill tosses me his card and I almost sprint away from the overeager local who, as Mrs Bevan said, can't appear to take his eyes off me.

CHAPTER 11

J have found sanctuary in a heavenly shop filled with things I need in my life as a matter of urgency.

I look around with pleasure at the shelves of reed diffusers, soaps, jewellery, scarves, and household decorative objects.

Finally, I can breathe again because this shop is just the tonic I need.

"Good afternoon."

I look up and smile at the lovely woman who is regarding me through curious eyes, and she smiles. "Hi, I'm Harriett Marshall. Welcome to Valley gifts."

"Eliza, I'm pleased to meet you."

"You must be new to Dream Valley. I never forget a face."

She looks more interested than nosey, and I nod. "I'm staying at Rock House for the summer, possibly longer."

"Ah."

Understanding dawns in her eyes. "You must be the new housekeeper for our celebrity visitor. I've heard a lot about you."

"Really?" I'm curious because I don't think I'm that interesting and I don't miss the twinkle in her eye. "I'm friends with Sammy

Jo, and she told me she was helping you. I must say, I'm impressed."

"You are?" I'm not sure what she's impressed about, and she nods. "Heading off to live with a stranger is very brave. I hope everything works out; you deserve it."

"I do." I smile, but inwardly I'm feeling on edge again. I know it's a small town, but I appear to be the gossip provider and I'm not used to that. In London, I blend in with the blurred scenery as the people rush past on their urgent business. Here it's a whole different ball game and I'm starting to understand a little of what Bill lives with every day.

"So, how can I help you, or are you just browsing?"

"Actually, I've been sent to gather air fresheners or similar. Anything that will scent a house, making it appear clean and sanitised."

Harriett points to the diffuser display. "Our home selection is on display there. All price points catered for, and I give a ten percent discount for three purchases or more."

Heading to the display, I pick out three, all the same scent and head to the counter.

"You didn't want a variety?" she says with a questioning look.

"No, they would all clash, and I just want one clean smell to waft around the house. Pure linen seems up to the job, so I think I'll start with that."

"Good choice. It's very popular."

As she rings up the purchase, she says casually, "What's Bill Monroe like? I must say, he's very easy on the eye."

"He's a sweetheart, and I genuinely mean that."

"That's good." She wraps them in tissue paper before placing them in a pretty paper carrier.

"That will be £54, please."

Feeling guilty, I hand over Bill's card and her raised eyebrows make me a little concerned. "Um, he's outside if you need his pin number or something."

Harriet looks excited. "Maybe we should, for security reasons."

Sighing inside, I head to the door and wave at him from across the street. The small crowd of people around him are holding out their phones and I see him casually kick off from the car and say something to the crowd. Then he heads our way and I sense the excitement radiating from behind the counter.

As soon as he enters the shop, it feels full because his personality could fill the Albert Hall.

"Eliza, darling, do you need me to pay?"

He moves effortlessly to the counter and offers Harriett his hand. "Charmed, my dear. I'm Bill."

She blushes and grips his hand quickly, shaking it vigorously. "Harriett Marshall. I'm pleased to meet you, um, Bill."

He smiles as if she's the love of his life and I'm starting to understand the power of celebrity and the magnetism of the man who wears it so well.

I watch as he pays for the diffusers with a smile and a cheeky wink, and glances around him with interest.

"What a charming shop. My wife Julia would love it here and I'll make sure to bring her in to inflate your profits."

Harriett is almost hyperventilating and smiles with excitement. "I would love to meet her."

I'm not so sure I share her enthusiasm and remonstrate with myself for judging her in advance.

By the time Bill prises himself away from Harriett's counter and we leave the cosy little shop, I am feeling a little delirious with fear because tomorrow everything could change.

* * *

I'm up bright and early the next morning and make sure to dress appropriately. Mrs Jenkins has promised to drop a spare apron around when she comes to cook up a feast for the new arrivals, before they arrive, of course. Bill has locked himself in his study since six am and told me to fetch him a tray of muesli and Greek yoghurt for breakfast and I am preparing myself for judgement day because this visit must pass every test she can throw at me.

I haven't even thought about their son. He isn't a consideration in this at all and I'm pretty certain he'll be happy to play with himself, anyway.

I know these city types. A stockbroker, Bill said. They spend most days hiding behind the Financial Times or checking their stocks and shares on their laptops. I even went on a blind date with one once and he was so boring I actually fell asleep. It was a little embarrassing but, in my defence, it was after an extremely long day, and I hadn't slept much the night before. We went to a premiere in Leicester Square, and the film was so boring I nodded off halfway through and woke up with his hand up my skirt and his wet tongue in my ear. Needless to say, I was out of there in record speed and blocked him from my phone.

Making sure the house is spick and span, I wait for Mrs Jenkins and, on the dot of eleven, she rings the doorbell and I almost drag her inside.

Laughing, she shrugs from my grip and carefully removes a folded apron from her big shopper bag.

"As ordered, Eliza, washed and starched for the occasion."

"I'm so grateful, Dorothy." We are now on first-name terms because the hired help should stick together in solidarity and as she washes her hands, I wait for instruction.

We soon set to work and nutritional content is the buzz word of the day and soon Dorothy has rustled up an amazing salad, including rice and lentils, with a pomegranate dressing. There are dishes prepared of smoked fish and salmon that require a quick blast in the oven before serving on a bed of the pomegranate rice mix.

For dessert, she made a gorgeous lemon mousse with zero fat and to my surprise, it's loaded with taste. In fact, Dorothy Jenkins is worth her weight in gold because she achieves the impossible on a plate.

Once dinner is prepared, she sets to making small tasters to hand around with pre-dinner drinks. Nutritional snacks to place under glass domes and gorgeous little baklava to serve with the coffee. I actually hug her tight and weep tears of gratitude when she grabs her bag to leave, after promising me she'll be here at six in the morning to help prepare the breakfast, before she heads to Valley House for her own shift.

As I show her out, I can't thank her enough, and she smiles. "You've really come on leaps and bounds, Eliza. Take credit for what you've achieved. I'm guessing you could fend for yourself if you had to."

"Please, no." I look at her in horror and she laughs softly. "Don't worry, I'm still here for you, but give yourself a pat on the back. You've learned more than you realise."

I wish I had her confidence, but I accept the compliment and wave her off from the front door.

As soon as her car disappears from view, I race back inside and head to my room to change.

If Bill wants a professional housekeeper, that's exactly what he's going to get and as I dress in my bodycon black dress, with my black tights, I congratulate myself on having the tools of the trade at my disposal. Admittedly, it's a little figure hugging and shorter than it should be, but the white starched apron will cover all that and as I tie the bow with a flourish, I admire my reflection with pride.

Yes. I look the part, a little more French maid than I would have liked, but they'll get the point.

Tying my brown hair in a bun on top of my head, I scrape back my fringe and make sure not a hair is loose because if I have to wear a hairnet, my street cred will be destroyed forever. The only black shoes I have is my stilettos which I can't wear if I want to walk anywhere, so I settle for my white trainers, practical although a little dirty in parts.

Now I feel good about myself. I think I have a couple of hours to go over this house again and make sure that nothing is out of place. For once, I feel in control. Dorothy has faith in me, Bill does too, and now I'm beginning to think I can actually pull this off.

Let Julia Monroe do her worst. I'm ready for whatever she hits me with.

CHAPTER 12

$\mathcal{T}$hey arrive at four o'clock on the dot. Bill received advanced warning by text, and we are standing waiting as the large Bentley rolls into the driveway. It feels as if royalty is visiting and as I stand nervously beside Bill, I feel my palms sweating and I hope to God she doesn't want to shake my hand.

Bill keeps smirking at me, probably because I've pulled out all the stops to look the part and his loud laughter was the first thing he did when he saw me for the first time. "Priceless, absolutely priceless, good for you."

I'm not sure what he meant about that, but the moment is upon us as the door flies open and a man steps out from the driver's side. He doesn't even look our way and heads around to the passenger door, and I hold my breath as Julia Monroe steps from the car in all her regal glory.

"Bill, darling."

Her loud voice wafts across the space, and he moves from my side to greet her with his arms outstretched.

"Darling, it's so good to see you."

I watch in awe as she falls against him and as his arms wrap around her, he kisses the top of her head and as I feel their emotion, it brings tears to my eyes. They are in love. It's obvious. She is clinging on tightly and he is no different.

Raising my eyes to the second occupant of the car, I almost take a step back because I was not expecting this.

Leaning against the door, looking like every woman's leading man, is a man who was first in line for looks. Tall, dark, and handsome doesn't do this man justice. His hair is short at the sides and slightly longer on top, framing the most bewitching light blue eyes. His casual clothing is different from how I imagined him, thinking he'd show up in a suit or something. Not a leather jacket and jeans that cling to his legs like a desperate woman.

His white t-shirt is sporting a popular brand logo and his boots look expensive. But it's the arrogant expression on his face that ruins the perfect package as he looks at the scene with a hint of irritation. Then he looks at me and the derision in his eyes gets my back up immediately and I pointedly look away because despite how amazing he looks, I hate him on sight.

"Darling, come and meet Eliza." Bill extricates himself from his wife's grip and, with a casual arm flung around her shoulder, he drags her across to greet me. Weirdly, I drop a slight curtsey, which causes him to laugh out loud and wink at me.

"Oh Eliza, darling, I've heard so much about you already. Come and give me a hug."

She throws out her arms and beckons me inside, and to say I'm shocked is an understatement. I wasn't expecting this.

Smothered by expensive perfume and slightly crushed by arms that definitely work out, I am clasped to her chest, and she actually kisses me on the cheek for what feels like fifty times.

"Gorgeous, darling. I'm so happy to meet you. Blake..."

She says loudly, directing her voice behind her. "Fetch our bags in. I need a drink, pronto."

I wonder if I should help with the bags, but before I can offer, she links her arm with mine and drags me inside with Bill leading the way.

"Guide me to the kitchen, darling. I'm so thirsty I could expire at any moment."

She whispers as he moves out of earshot, "I don't suppose you have any gin lurking around here? If you do, I'd be grateful if you could slip a shot in my tonic water — on the sly, of course."

She grins and all my worries melt away in one relieved burst of thank God she's normal.

She carries on in a low voice, "Bill isn't supposed to drink, which is why I keep it hidden. Poor man, I don't want to rub it in."

This is news to me, and I wonder if she knows her husband is obviously ignoring that advice.

"Leave it with me."

I don't know what else to say and as she heads into the kitchen, she sweeps the room with a critical eye.

"Well, this looks ok, I suppose."

Moving around the room, she opens cupboards and peers inside. I hold my breath as she moves to the fridge and share an anxious look with Bill as she regards the contents, and then her sigh of relief is echoed by two more.

"Nice to see a healthy fridge. Well done, Eliza."

She turns and smiles, and I thank God for the miracle of Dorothy Jenkins.

Quickly, I head to the cupboard to arrange some drinks and reach for three tumblers.

"Would you like ice in your drinks?"

I ask as a collective and Julia nods, "Super darling, although I must check that you've used filtered water and a tumbler isn't really a suitable vessel for a long, satisfying drink. Maybe a goblet would suffice on this occasion."

"Um..." I don't know what to say and Bill chips in. "It's already filtered. They have a system, apparently."

This is news to me, but I'll run with it and Julia nods with approval. "Good. I'm glad to see they are up to date in Dream Valley."

I'm not sure how I can slip a gin into the tonic because the bottle is in the garage and I'm anxious about that. It doesn't seem right doing things furtively, but I'll do anything to get Julia on side, so I say with a smile, "I could serve your drinks in the living room if you like. The sun is still high, and it floods the room with light."

Julia smiles happily. "What an amazing suggestion. Come on, Bill, you can show me around while Eliza fixes our drinks and then tell me all about your screenplay."

They head off holding hands and I waste no time in racing to the garage to retrieve the bottle of gin. The trouble is, as soon as I exit the room, I run into a wall, literally.

Strong arms close around me and it takes my brain a moment to catch up and then I realise this wall has a beating heart and smells rather divine and then it speaks with a low, angry growl. "Slow down. You'll hurt yourself and everyone around you if you're not careful."

Pulling away quickly, I take a step back and stutter, "I, I, I'm sorry."

He looks at me as if I'm an irritant that he could do without engaging with and just puffs out an exasperated breath and heads into the kitchen, leaving me feeling like a worthless piece of dirt under his shoe.

Silently fuming, I head to the garage and after locating the bottle of gin, conveniently hidden in a bucket, I unscrew the cap and swig a bracing shot of courage to get me through this.

Tucking the bottle away into my apron, I head back to the kitchen and my heart sinks when I see him making a coffee.

"Oh, um, I can do that for you."

I'm not being polite. I just want him the hell out of my

kitchen, and he looks at me with another irritated stare and growls, "I doubt it."

"Excuse me."

I'm confused because it's almost as if he knows how challenged I am in all things domestic already.

He jerks his head to the machine and says in an emotionless voice, "From the look of this machine, it hasn't been used. This tells me that you haven't either worked it out yet, or don't make coffee this way. Knowing my father, he would be happy with what comes out of a jar, so I'm guessing you have taken the easy option. I, however, have very particular coffee requirements that require skill and an understanding of the process. Therefore, I will make my own coffee, how I like it, and spare you the humiliation of getting it wrong."

I am speechless. The fact he turns away without waiting for an answer, effectively dismissing me, gets my back up immediately. But how can I argue with him because that machine scares the life out of me, and I wouldn't even know where the 'on' switch is? On this occasion, he is right, and I would be a fool to challenge him, so I shrug it off and just add it to the pile of reasons why I already hate this man and briefly wonder if he was adopted because how did he come from the two lovely people who are no longer in this room?

So, I take my cue from him and pointedly ignore him and just carry on as if he isn't here. If he wants conversation from me, he's going to have to shape up because I will not be treated like this by anyone.

I can feel him watching me, though, which is uncomfortable for many reasons. Firstly, how on earth do I add a shot of gin to Julia's drink all the time he's here? Instead, I fuss around setting the tray and am grateful for the small appetisers Dorothy whipped up and, as I take great pleasure in making the tray look pretty, I hope he takes the hint and leaves so I can finish the job.

Sadly, my wish is denied because he just grabs his coffee and kicks out the bar stool before perching on the edge, his long legs stretched out as he watches me with an unreadable expression. It feels slightly disconcerting because the silence speaks volumes. Is he waiting for me to engage him in conversation, or doesn't he feel the need to speak to the hired help? I'm not sure what to do, so I do nothing and just carry on feeling every look, every breath he takes, and every thought in his head as he watches me.

Finally, all is ready aside from the gin and with two hands on the tray, I make to leave, hoping I get a chance to add it in the other room before Julia and Bill make it there.

As I turn to leave, however, a low drawl stops me in my tracks. "Have you forgotten something?"

My skin prickles like a thousand knives scraping away my sanity and I say sharply, "I don't think so."

He growls,"Word of advice. Keep my mother happy. I believe she gave you instructions that you have either ignored or forgotten. Either one is foolish and won't make for a good start."

"I don't know what you mean?"

I stare at him with a blank look, trying to brazen it out and the slight sneer on his face gets my back up. "My mother prefers gin with her tonic, as I'm sure she explained."

"How do you know?" He raises his eyes and I splutter, "I mean, you weren't there."

His low laugh has no trace of humour in it, and he leans forward and says in a deep voice, "I know my mother and it would have been the first request she made. Why don't you allow me?"

To my horror, he unfolds himself from the barstool like a pouncing panther and slips his hand between the tray and into my pocket, closing his fingers around the bottle of gin I thought was hidden. With a smirk, he stares into my eyes and despite myself, I can't look away and watch as he slowly unscrews the cap and proceeds to add a splash to both drinks on the tray. Then he screws the cap back on and slips the bottle back in my pocket and smirks. "Now you can go."

Feeling the heat rising in my cheeks, I turn and stumble from the room because what was that? How did he know? Is he a mind reader in his spare time?

I feel mortified, on the wrong foot and out of my depth, but most of all I feel intoxicated by him, which is not a good thing for any of us. Blake Monroe is a hazard in my life, and, like all hazards, I am keeping as far away from him as possible.

CHAPTER 13

J head off to deliver my drinks, silently fuming. Why is Blake such an arrogant idiot when his father is so sweet and amazing? His mother is a lot nicer than I anticipated, too, so the only reason I can think of is he's adopted.

More than anything, I hate my reaction to him. Like a snake charmer he held me captive with those hypnotic eyes, and it felt as if I was waiting for something; I'm not sure what, but there's something compelling about him and it's now imperative that I keep my distance.

"Ah, there she is." Bill calls out as I stagger into the room with my tray, and he heads across like a true gentleman and takes it from me.

"Allow me."

He offers me a reassuring smile and I am so glad I can count on him to lift my mood.

Julia is standing by the bifold doors and says with awe, "The pictures online didn't do this place justice. I must say I'm blown away, darling. This is the perfect place to take time out and reconnect with your inner goddess."

Bill rolls his eyes at me, and I stem the giggle that would give the game away and Julia says loudly, "Eliza, come and chat to me. Did you bring yourself a drink? We should toast happy times ahead."

I head towards her and say guiltily, "It's fine. I'm not thirsty."

"Nonsense darling, thirst has nothing to do with it. Bill…" She turns her head and says sharply, "Fetch Eliza a gin and tonic and find out where Blake is skulking at. We should all be present for the toast."

My skin crawls like a swarm of bees are threatening to sting at the mention of their son's name, and I try desperately to focus on his mother instead.

Julia Monroe is absolutely gorgeous. I would have expected no less, given how lovely Bill is. She has shoulder-length blonde hair that is cut sharply, with a blunt fringe that frames her stunning blue eyes. Her figure is well toned and her make-up 'beauty counter' perfect, which shows she certainly knows her way around a mascara wand and a primer. She is wearing narrow cut, tailored trousers, with a white blouse, and a smart jacket to finish the look off. Her mirrored shades are still perched on top of her head and the scent she's wearing is absolutely delightful.

I think I'm a little in love with Julia Monroe because she is every inch perfect. She apparently has high standards though, as she casts her eye across the outside space and says thoughtfully, "I wonder how often the gardener visits. I mean, those weeds look as if they've had the run of the place for several days already and I'm certain there are still some leaves congregating by the pots over there."

Shaking her head, she sighs. "I'll get onto the agent in the morning. Once you let the small things slide, the place goes to wrack and ruin."

Feeling slightly guilty about that, although I don't know why, I stutter, "I could…"

She holds up her hand. "I'm not expecting you to be a jack of all trades, darling. The house is your domain, and I can see you've got that under control. Now, we should discuss the menu and make a list of anything you need. I require a full report and assurance that Bill is sticking to his regime."

His regime. Briefly wondering if that involves several gin and tonics, a whole bottle of wine and enough sugar to fill a chocolate factory. I certainly hope it's not anything but that because that's the only regime I can think of.

With a sinking feeling, I can tell I'm going to have to do some quick thinking just to spare him the lecture that doesn't seem that far away.

I can feel him even before I see him and Julia says, "There you are. Come inside and we'll get to know Eliza. I need to know absolutely everything about her and hope she won't mind my questions."

Questions. I'm now very much on edge and she points to a seat by the window and says quickly, "Sit there, darling. Bill, where's Eliza's drink?"

Bill springs forward with an apologetic smile and winks as he hands me the glass, mouthing 'sorry' before he retreats to the sofa.

Blake lowers his impressive body into a chair facing mine and studies me with a long, lazy look that causes the heat to build and the nerves to take over.

Julia perches next to Bill and says pleasantly, "Isn't this perfectly lovely? I must say, Dream Valley is shaping up nicely."

"You haven't even seen it yet. Reserve judgement until you have."

Blake's derisive drawl causes his mother to raise her eyes and stare at him with an irritated look. "First impressions count for a lot, Blake, and the ones here are good. If this was a run-down hovel with sub-standard cleanliness, I would have a different opinion, but it's not. It's modern, clean, and charming. The view is breath-taking and the road here devoid of potholes and speed bumps. There was no traffic or litter that I saw, and the road signs were clean and easily read.

Blake snorts and I stare at Julia in utter amazement. Who checks road signs for cleanliness? This is a first.

Bill runs his arm along the back of her chair and laughs out loud. "Oh, how I've missed you, darling."

It's quite sweet how her face blushes with a hint of pink and her eyes shine as she looks at him fondly. "Of course, you have Bill. I would be worried if you haven't."

For a moment, they shut us out and share a tender moment that gives me hope that there are some couples who never lose that loving feeling. Not that I've ever had it myself, I mean, not true love. Definitely not that.

My dating life is courtesy of an app called Hinge and all it does is unhinge me after every date. There was the guy from Potters Bar who thought he was a cowboy and called me sugar and wore a Stetson. It was embarrassing to walk into the Pizza Express with him because I'm not sure the spurs on his cowboy boots were strictly necessary to enjoy some dough balls and a meat feast.

Then there was the computer programmer from Morden who tapped his fingers nervously on the table as if he was imputing vital information into a spreadsheet. He had a nervous twitch too and halfway through the Nando's, removed one of those pill compartment boxes and began counting out his meds, before washing them down with a 'tap water please' and moaning about how stressful his life was.

There have been some normal ones too but for some reason I never clicked with any of them and the odd occasion where I did see them again, it was embarrassing to decline their offer of a quick one in the back seat of the car in a multi-story on the way home. No, this is exactly why I needed to change it up a little and seeing how happy Bill and Julia are, has hardened my resolve. I will accept nothing less than my soulmate or remain a spinster until the end. I will be true to myself and not settle for second best because somewhere out there is my soulmate, just waiting for the stars to align and the planets to collide.

"Blake. Do you have any questions for Eliza?"

Julia's sharp voice brings me back into the room and I jump as his deep, husky voice carries across.

"No."

"None at all." Julia sounds surprised, but he just sounds bored as he says bluntly, "Why would I?"

Julia sighs. "Forgive my son, Eliza, the only interest he shows is in making money and making more money. Maybe one day something more worthwhile will catch his attention. A mother can hope at least."

She stares at me with a soul-searching look. "So, Bill tells me you are an amazing cook and great company. You leave him to work and make sure he has regular snacks and fetch him drinks to keep his mind active."

"I'm not geriatric yet?" Bill says with amusement and Julia laughs, "Of course not, darling, you're at that distinguished stage of life."

"Is that what they call it?"

"Me, on the other hand…" Julia smirks. "I'm in my prime."

"Of course you are, darling." Bill laughingly pulls her against him, and she giggles as he kisses the top of her head. Pushing him away, she fixes me with an amused grin. "When I say prime, I mean I've worked out what I want from life and make sure I accept nothing less. I have a strict regime that I follow like a religion. I'm happily settled with a man I adore, and I have a son who I am immensely proud of, although I would be even prouder if he settled down at last and stopped drifting."

I steal a look at her drifting son and love how he rolls his eyes and looks bored. In fact, baiting Blake could be a new hashtag and I would happily contribute to the pile on an hourly basis just to see that spark of annoyance flash more frequently across his arrogant features.

Julia leans forward and stares at me hard, making me feel a little hot under the collar.

"So, Bill tells me you want a new beginning. Tell me about the old one."

Bill smiles his encouragement and I take a deep breath.

"I used to work for a solicitor in London, just off Bond Street."

"Impressive." Julia looks as if she approves and says quickly, "Go on."

"Well, I suppose I thought I'd made it. I mean, not many of my friends had such high-profile jobs, but I soon discovered I was just an admin assistant. My boss would sit on an elevated desk before us, and we would work under his fierce glare until our regimented breaks. My co-worker had been there thirty years and I suppose it took one particular last will and testament to make my mind up for me."

"This sounds interesting." Julia leans forward and Bill grins. "It's a good one."

He winks at me, giving me the courage to continue and as I take a sip of my drink, courtesy of Blake, I nearly spit out the pure gin that fills the glass.

My eyes water as I stare at him in shock and he just smirks and leans back in his chair and says, "Yes, go on, Eliza."

Feeling as if my face is on fire, I wish there was a glass of water handy to douse the flames, either that or the smug look on his face, but I resort to just turning away from him and fixing Julia with my sweetest smile.

"Well, it all started with Annalise Turtle."

Blake coughs, but I don't give him the satisfaction of my attention.

"Anyway, she made it her mission to marry men for money."

Julia looks a little uncomfortable about this, and Bill takes her hand and kisses it in a sweet gesture of affection.

"She was good at her job and soon had more money than each of her previous husbands. She chose older men who didn't have long and began a career of materialism and wealth that took her to foreign countries, mixing with celebrities and living in palatial homes."

Julia looks worried. "And you want to be like this Turtle woman?"

"Good God, no." I shake my head vigorously. "I'm not saying I agree with what she did, but I admired her for sticking to her plan. Anyway, she soon became the older wealthy woman and took a string of partners with the same thing in mind. A role reversal of sorts and she was the master of the game. She didn't let anyone get too comfortable and just enjoyed their attention until she moved onto the next one."

Julia has turned white and says slowly, "Darling, I don't think…"

"Let her finish, mum." Blake leans forward, his elbows on his knees and the look in his eyes should terrify me. His eyes have darkened and there's an aura of danger surrounding him that I would be a fool to ignore.

Taking another swig of neat gin, I decide to run with fool because I say brightly, "Anyway, when she died, she left all the money to a homeless shelter in Liverpool. The city she was born. They got to benefit from the money that she amassed over time, and some would argue it was the right thing to do. I suppose what I'm trying to say is that Annalise Turtle embraced the unconventional. She took risks and enjoyed a life many of us will never experience. It made me look at my own life and decide to shake it up a little, and then I saw Bill's advert. It was fate, I guess, and so here I am now. Free of the desk, standing at a crossroads, and I'm not sure where it leads, but at least I'm now the master of my own destiny."

Julia says slowly, "Um, lovely darling, but what I don't under-stand is, what next? I mean, Bill will head back to Wimbledon in a few months' time, so what will Eliza do when the contract's up?"

There's a sharpness to her tone that tells me she's thinking the worst of me, and I say quickly, "I have six months' salary left to move onto the next adventure. Maybe I'll go abroad, volunteer to build an orphanage, go grape picking in France, who knows? The important thing is I made the decision to change my life, and this is the beginning of that. I have no ending, just a starting point and I owe it all to Bill."

Julia looks sharply at her husband, who nods in agreement. "You've got to hand it to her, darling. She's a brave one. I like that in a person. She reminds me of myself all those years ago when I defied my parents and took to the stage. I'm definitely cheering her on."

"Of course," Julia smiles. "We all wish you the very best of luck. Anyway, I'm feeling rather tired now. I don't suppose we could eat and then I'll enjoy a leisurely bath and an early night."

Jumping up, I feel a little unsteady on my feet and slur a little, "Of corsh. Leave it wissh me."

The room blurs a little as I stagger towards the door, and I regret downing what ended up as a whole tumbler of neat gin. I vow to never accept a drink from a stranger ever again because if I can manage to rustle up a gourmet evening meal without ruining it somehow, this could be the beginning of my new life and the end.

CHAPTER 14

*F*eeling my way along the hall, I make it to the kitchen and lean against the counter, willing the room to stop spinning. This is a disaster. Briefly I wonder if I should put out a SOS to Mrs Jenkins. She could pop up in a cloud of white smoke and save me from myself like all good fairy godmothers.

As I take deep breaths, I'm surprised when out of nowhere, a strong hand holds the back of my head and I feel a cool glass resting against my lips. Then a deep voice says firmly, "Drink this."

Realising it's the drink doctoror, I clamp my mouth tightly shut and shake my head vigorously and then am astonished when two fingers prise it open and cold clear water makes its way down my throat, making me cough.

"What the…"

"I said drink this. It will help."

Despite myself, I seize the glass gratefully and gulp down the remaining water and then feel him take my hand and guide me onto one of the barstools.

"Lie against the cool marble. It will stop your head spinning."

"Did you drug me?" I slur my words as I collapse on the counter, loving the cool stone against my cheek.

"No, I gave you courage to face my mother."

"I didn't need your help."

I close my eyes and feel my head spinning and hear a low voice whisper near my ear, "You needed to relax. She doesn't tolerate weakness or nerves in anyone. I did you a favour."

"You reckon."

I groan as I feel my face throbbing with heat and my mind moving at a hundred miles an hour.

"You've sabotaged me. She'll fire me if I don't serve up a gourmet, low calorie, fat-free meal containing every power food there is."

A low chuckle surprises me and he says huskily, "You're not as stupid as you look."

"Excuse me." I try to lift my head and he says firmly, "Stay there. Leave this with me and just try to get yourself together to serve the bloody food."

I don't argue because all I want to do is sleep off this alcohol poisoning because it must be. It was only one glass of the hard stuff and I'm not that much of a lightweight, surely. Then again, I am exactly that person because I must pass out and the next thing I know, I wake to the most divine smell of cooking which makes my mouth water. My head feels heavy as I lift it and opening one eye, see something that confirms I've had far too much to drink and am hallucinating.

Blake is standing at the range cooker, stirring a pot of something that smells divine and as the room swims into focus, I see an array of plates and bowls of salad, all neatly waiting to be served.

As I gasp in surprise, he turns around and his amused grin immediately resurrects me because I am ashamed of myself. The enemy who brought me to my knees has taken over my kitchen and I must fight to protect my authority here.

So, with a heavy head, I drag myself up to a sitting position and take a few energising breaths and test out my power of speech.

"Thank you, Master Monroe. I'll take it from here."

"Master." He smirks. "I like the sound of that."

"I mean…" Blinking frantically, I say, "In a junior Monroe capacity, of course, not as in, well, you know, the other sense of the word."

"Which is?"

"You know perfectly well what it is, or you wouldn't have made it into this big point scoring drama."

Maybe it's the adrenalin in me, but suddenly I'm firing on all cylinders and smooth down my apron and say briskly, "Ok, thank you. I think I feel better now, and I appreciate your help in my medical emergency."

"Is that what it was?"

"You know it was." Feeling the heart rising in my face, I turn away and say loudly, "OK, you can take your seat and I'll serve the starter salad. If you want to make yourself useful, you can take a jug of water with the filtered ice cubes into the other room."

"OK."

I'm amazed when he places the spoon down and turns to grab the jug and does exactly what I said.

As he leaves the room, I congratulate myself on effectively dismissing him and sending him on his way, and I look around, trying to get my head back in the game.

Venturing over to the pot on the stove, I relish the smell of something that makes my mouth water. It looks and smells fantastic and spying the steamed rice on the side, I am happy that everything is covered.

Turning down the gas, proving to myself that I am improving in leaps and bounds, I hum a happy tune as I prepare to carry the salads through on a tray.

Feeling like a domesticated goddess, I glide into the room and see the table has been laid already and the candles lit and silently thank Julia for stepping in. The lighting has dimmed, and gentle music plays in the background, and I look around with pleasure. This is nice. A soft relaxing meal for one of the nicest families I have ever met, son excluded and as I set the salads down on the placemats, I wonder if I should shout 'dinner's ready'. I'm guessing they are changing into evening wear or something. Maybe people in Wimbledon dress for dinner.

I wonder if I should see if Valley Marketplace has a bell or something that I could use. Either that or a gong would be good.

The jug of water is on the table, but there is no sign of their arrogant son. I can't even bring myself to think of his name and for a moment, I'm unsure what to do.

Then I hear a low drawl coming from the doorway. "Take a seat."

Peering across the room, I make out Blake looking quite dashing in sweatpants and a tightly fitted t-shirt and I say in confusion, "I'm sorry, I can eat in the kitchen. It's ok. Um, where are Bill and Julia and why are there only two place settings?"

I'm wondering if I've stumbled into a parallel world and step back a little as Blake moves closer and says with amusement, "They went to bed hours ago."

"They couldn't have. What are you talking about?"

I am so confused, and he points to the clock on the mantle-piece. "You passed out for a few hours and it's now eleven pm."

"Are you serious?" I stare at him in utter shock and his eyes gleam as he guides me into the nearby chair and leans in, whispering, "It's fine. I served up the food in the fridge and told them you were busy in the kitchen. I covered for you, you're welcome."

"But…" My mind isn't functioning right now as I look at the intimate meal for two and say nervously, "But this…"

"Is for you. I made you something to soak up the alcohol and you need to eat to avoid a hangover in the morning."

"But you don't cook; you don't do anything. Bill told me."

I'm babbling, but I'm in shock and he shrugs. "Just because I don't, it doesn't mean I can't."

He stands and fixes me with a stern look. "Drink the water and eat the power food." He actually winks and says over his shoulder, "I'll be right back."

I'm glad there's a chair handy because I don't think my legs can support me anymore and I look at the rather romantic table and blink rapidly several times. My stomach growls angrily. Probably because of the abuse it's suffered and on autopilot, I spear a forkful of leaves that are coated in a citrus dressing and then stare at the plate in puzzled bewilderment because Dorothy never made this dressing. I would know if she had because I absolutely love this and would have made it my number one lunch, dinner, and breakfast probably.

I start cramming as many leaves into my mouth as possible, like a grazing cow, and look up slightly guiltily when Blake heads into the room, carrying a basket of rolls and saying with satisfaction, "Good, you've started."

Feeling slightly guilty about that because where are my manners? I gaze at him from under my lashes and whisper, "Why?"

He sets the rolls down before me and I love the scent of hot decadent bread wafting through my senses, making my mouth water. Bread has a habit of being able to do that, or it could be the man serving it. I can't stop staring at him because the strong arms that flex across the table at me as he reaches for one of the rolls would look good wrapped around me. The slight stubble on his chiselled face makes him appear rough and caveman like, which has the woman in me screaming to get to him and the lazy way those eyes are regarding me, makes me want him despite what my head is telling me and then it dawns on me that he is eating too.

"I thought you would have eaten with your parents."

"I did."

"But…"

He shrugs. "I don't like to eat alone, so I figured you wouldn't either."

Something shatters inside me that I'm not sure I'll be able to repair, no matter how much I want to. The hate I was feeling towards him has mysteriously disappeared and the interest is growing – fast.

I don't want to like him. He's obnoxious, rude and makes me feel inferior, but these small acts of kindness smooth those rough edges and spark an interest that has no business being there. Then he ruins it all by smirking and saying with an amused grin, "Are you always this chaotic?"

"What do you mean?"

"Well, since the moment I arrived, you appear to have been trying a little too hard. From the whole French maid outfit and the appearance of being able to do your job, when in reality we can both see you're struggling."

I'm now really concerned because if he sees the truth, then so must his mother and I shiver inside as he leans back and casually strips me bare with just one look.

"We, as in you and me"

Just hearing me referenced in the same sentence as him causes me to break out in a hot flush and I stutter, "I don't know what you're talking about."

Leaning forward, he stares at me like an investigating officer in a murder trial. "It's ok, I don't judge."

"Not much." I snap because immediately I'm on the defensive and I hate that he just raises his eyes and looks amused. "Your little story about the gold digger has my mother in a frenzy."

The fork of salad doesn't make it into my mouth as it freezes in mid-air and I whisper, "She's what?"

"She thinks you have designs on my father and called an emergency meeting over dinner."

I set the fork down and look at him in horror. He is obviously enjoying this revelation because he smirks and his eyes flash as he says with a smirk, "She believes you are after his money to kickstart your career."

"Does Bill think that too?" The tears smart behind my eyes because I'm hating every minute of this. Just the thought they think so badly of me makes me want to cry and Blake has the emotional capacity of a wet wipe as he shrugs, "No but it's not him you need to convince if you want to keep your job."

This is a disaster, and I don't know how to handle it and Blake says coolly, "I'll fetch the main course. We need a plan of action."

"We do?" I'm wishing I hadn't woken up now. Maybe I didn't, and this is just one of those weird dreams that makes no sense and causes your heart to pound in the middle of the night, waking you up in a cold sweat. Yes, this is exactly that and as I go into full dream like panic mode, his amused voice cuts through my hysteria. "What are you doing?"

Looking down, I see my fingers frantically pinching my arm and whisper, "Trying to wake myself up."

His low laughter is not welcome here, and he scrapes back his chair and grins. "You need more food; the alcohol is obviously still in charge of your brain."

I don't even have the energy to flash back a brilliant retort, because I may as well pack now. Why did I blurt out that story? Of course it looks bad. A gold digger. A career gold digger even. That's exactly what Julia thinks and probably reluctantly, Bill, too. I feel so upset I'm not sure I can ever look at them again and then the salad calls my name and smiles up at me with compassion, begging me to eat it to make myself feel better.

Slowly, I chew on the miracle food and contemplate my options. I could go back to Pemberley Thomson, or I could stick pins in my eyes. Neither one is appealing, so I think about where I am now. Possibly, I could find a job here in Dream Valley. Maybe Dorothy needs an apprentice. Mrs Bevan might need staff and I'd even tolerate Gerry if it meant I didn't have to go home and admit to my mum that I've embarrassed her in front of her screen idol.

Blake returns, carrying more food from the gods and he sets the plate down and says in his commanding voice, "Eat this and listen. I have a plan."

"You do?" I stare at him in surprise, and he nods, retreating to his own seat and nodding towards the food.

"Eat up and I'll fill you in."

I need no further invitation because the smell of this dish is enough for me to ditch the cutlery and just fall face first into it. I am so hungry in my time of trauma, which is odd, really. I thought emotional trauma made you lose your appetite, not gorge on everything in sight, thinking it's miracle food. I have definitely had too much to drink, especially as I'm waiting to hear Blake's plan and am even hoping it's one I can adopt.

However, my appetite deserts me in a heartbeat as he says, "We start dating."

CHAPTER 15

*T*here are moments in life where you think you fell asleep and missed a big section of it. Where your memory struggles to keep up and remind you what happened in what must be a brain malfunction. A blackout of the cognitive kind, because why is this Blake's great plan? It's almost laughable.

He watches my reaction carefully and seems almost amused as I stare at him in shock. "We what?"

My voice shakes as I seek confirmation that my ears are paying tricks on me and he says casually, "We start dating. That way mum relaxes, and you keep your job."

"But..." I blink rapidly and that's all I can say because it's obvious my mind has decided it no longer wants to be part of my life and has left me already.

"It's easy. We spend time together and then declare we have fallen madly in love. Mum breathes a sigh of relief; Dad keeps his partner in crime. You keep your job and may just become better at it by the end of the contract."

The fact he's insulting my domestic skills can be dealt with later because the one thing screaming inside my head is the fact he wants me to 'date' him.

"But…"

"You're welcome." He starts eating the food and looks as if he's enjoying the situation as well as the food and I say weakly, "Why are you doing this?"

"Why not?"

"That's not an answer. It's another question." Once again, this man irritates me even in kindness, and he grins. "I have my reasons."

"That you'd like to share, perhaps."

"No."

I feel like screaming. This man is infuriating in a very sexy, screen idol, condescending, arrogant way. Why was he blessed with movie star looks and the personality of a bar of soap? You love the smell, want to rub it all over your body, but don't want to be seen talking to it? Pushing aside the fact he can seriously cook, appears to be a Samaritan coming to my aid in a crisis and quite honestly, personality aside, is quite a decent guy, I can only conclude that he has an ulterior motive and there is something he's not telling me.

"Eat up, it will get cold."

His command has me shovelling food into my mouth like a greedy pig and I don't care that he obviously finds it amusing because I need to get away from him and digest things along with a couple of rennies and an aspirin for my headache that's distracting me from calm, rational thought. Gin is now officially the devil's brew and I vow never to let a drop pass my lips again because inadvertently I have stumbled down a rabbit hole that is even crazier than the one in Wonderland.

Feeling decidedly weak in every way, I slump back in my chair and stare at the flickering candle. Its dance of pleasure taunts me because how dare that flame have such a good time when my life has taken a weird turn into cuckoo land.

Blake carries on eating and says casually, "So, in the morning after breakfast, I'll whisk you away on the premise of gathering provisions. Mum will enjoy some quality time with my father and when we return, we will have got closer."

"Closer?"

"Flirtatious looks, small smiles of secrecy, isn't that how it works?"

"You tell me, you appear to have it all figured out."

"I always do."

"Thanks, but no thanks."

I blurt it out like a petulant teenager and stare at him with a frosty look. "Listen, I know you mean well, but I'm not one to run away from my mistakes. I'll just apologise and reassure your mum in the morning. There you go, crisis averted, and we can carry on with our day."

Scraping my chair back, I smooth down my dress that appears to have risen to indecent levels and say with a bravery I'm certainly not feeling, "I'll tidy this away and leave you to retire for the night. You must be tired after the journey, which has obviously messed with your mind. So, thank you for the lovely meal and the help with my situation tonight — that you caused incidentally, but I'm prepared to let that one go with the promise you will never doctor my drink again."

I lift the empty plates from the table and head towards the kitchen and am grateful when he doesn't try to stop me. Date him, he has got to be kidding. Why is that the great master plan? He's obviously a voyeur, somebody who sees an opportunity and decides to take full advantage of it. I knew I shouldn't have worn this figure-hugging dress and told stories about gold diggers. It's obviously given him the green light to lure me into intimate relations with him. Just thinking of what that would involve makes me second guess my decision already. I mean, it has been a long time, and he is seriously gorgeous and rather sexy with the Heathcliff, caveman vibe he has going on, but I have my principles and tricking his lovely parents is not high on my to do list.

I am so fired up I actually manage to stack the dishwasher in some kind of order and then jump as he enters the room carrying the rest of the dishes. Setting them down on the counter, he says in his husky drawl, "Think about it. Give me your answer when you've had time to sleep on it. When you're ready, we can get started."

He turns and leaves the kitchen and I stare after him with my mouth slack against my jaw. He is serious. But why? I can't for one moment understand why he is doing this and the thing I hate the most is the fact I am even considering it because, for some reason, playing a cosy couple with him is not as unappealing as I thought it would be.

CHAPTER 16

*W*hen I wake the next morning, it's with a pounding head and a sense of doom. What happened last night? Did Blake really attend an emergency family meeting about my intentions towards his father and then proposition me after getting me drunk? Surely not.

I look around my room and note that everything looks the same, so I must have slept heavily and dreamt it.

However, my head is giving the game away and I gingerly touch it, wondering if I have somehow been poisoned by alcohol. It's a possibility, most definitely, and as I stagger to the ensuite bathroom, I stare at the face of Hades in the mirror and decide that today is the first day of the rest of my alcohol-free life.

Somehow, I make it down to the kitchen just before seven and my heart sinks when one very annoying alpha male is already there, stereotypically leafing through the Financial Times. I'm not even sure where he managed to rustle that up from. Knowing him, he probably had it flown in by carrier pigeon.

"Morning, Eliza."

"Is it?"

I stomp around the kitchen, regretting every minute of last

night except for that salad dressing. Surreptitiously, I look for a tell-tale bottle in the fridge when I open it, but all that's in there are the super food provisions and the remains of last night's meal.

Blake is nursing a cup of expertly made coffee–by him and looking as if he is deeply engrossed in world affairs.

I'm wondering how I can get him to leave, because Dorothy will be here soon to help me with the breakfast preparations.

"If you want to take that through to the dining table, I'll bring you a freshly squeezed orange juice if you like." I act as if the juice won't be straight from the Tetra Pak, and he looks over his newspaper and raises his eyes. "Freshly squeezed, you say."

Mentally kicking myself because, of course, he would pick up on that to beat me over the head with.

"Yes." I smile sweetly, hoping this is an end to the conversation, and he lowers the paper and says with a challenge in his voice, "I'd like to watch this."

"What?"

"You expertly squeezing the oranges."

"Then you'll be disappointed."

"I doubt it." His slow smile confuses me and, feeling a little flustered, I turn and start pulling dishes out of the cupboards in a very haphazard manner. "I did them earlier. You missed it."

"I see."

"Yes, I couldn't sleep, so I came downstairs to prepare what I could. Sorry. Maybe another day."

"And the container in the fridge was coincidentally on hand to store it in. That was lucky."

I should have known he was ferreting around the fridge again, and I bite my sharp retort and say lightly, "Yes, it was. Anyway, I really need my personal space. You see, I can't work with an audience and would appreciate it if you keep out of the domestic areas in the future."

"The domestic areas. You mean the kitchen, I presume."

"Yes, and possibly the utility room. I carry out housekeeping duties in there."

"Like what?" He leans his elbows on the island counter and watches me with a hint of amusement tugging at his lips.

"Oh, you know, washing, ironing, sweeping up and disinfecting."

"You do the whole house from there, impressive."

"Of course not." I roll my eyes as if he's stupid. "It's my command centre where I plan my day. I need it clear so I can concentrate. Sorry, but that's just how it is. Anyway, I'm sure it won't be a problem. I guess you're leaving later today to get back in time for work in the morning."

"That's where you're wrong."

"What do you mean?"

I hold my breath as he shrugs, obviously enjoying this exchange. "I'm working from here for the foreseeable future."

"You're what?" I'm astounded, and he grins. "Mum's taking the Bentley back to Wimbledon tonight. She has many social engagements she's committed to. I am working from home on a particular project and may as well do it here."

"But I thought the whole point of this was that Bill was given space. What does he think about it?"

"It was his suggestion."

I have no words and Dorothy chooses the moment to head through the back door, saying loudly, "The cavalry's arrived."

Blake raises his eyes and I blush as if I've been caught in a comprising position and as she heads into the room, Dorothy says with surprise, "Oh, you have visitors. I'm sorry to interrupt."

"He's not a visitor, he's…"

"Eliza's boyfriend. I'm pleased to meet you."

He holds out his hand and I stare at him in mortified shock as Dorothy winks at me and doesn't just take his hand, she seizes it and I wonder if she'll ever give it back.

By the time he wrestles it from her grasp, he turns to face a frozen statue because I couldn't move if I tried. My boyfriend–since when.

He saunters like a panther across the room, leaning down, whispers, "Check mate, Eliza. I'll keep your secret and you keep your job. I think we'll make the perfect couple."

"Why?" I whisper the word because it's all I can think of and his mouth grazes against my ear as he says huskily, "Why not?"

He leaves the room sucking all the oxygen with him and I am more confused than ever. Why is he doing this? It doesn't make sense and Dorothy is no help because she fans herself and says in a low voice, "Wow, he's gorgeous. I wish I was you right now."

"I wish you were me, too."

I really don't understand Blake Monroe, and the thought of being blackmailed into some sort of twisted arrangement with him isn't making my head feel any better.

Dorothy gets straight to it and starts amassing enough food to feed a small army, all perfectly healthy, of course, made with the most natural ingredients. All I can do is assist her and watch, trying desperately to learn, so at least when I'm arrested for killing their son, I'll get a job in the prison kitchen and serve out my stretch on easy street.

CHAPTER 17

*J*ulia enters the dining room like a breath of fresh air. I say dining room, it's actually a section in the large open plan living room that makes up several zoned areas of relaxation. Weirdly, the table has been set already with a white tablecloth and even a flower in a glass jar. I'm wondering if Dorothy isn't the only fairy godmother around here because it's as if magic is aiding my quest to become the perfect housekeeper.

Blake is chatting to Bill near the bifold doors and looks to be in an easy conversation. Bill laughs and then looks around and spies his wife entering the room and I love the huge smile that breaks out when he sees her.

"Darling, it's a glorious morning. We should take a walk."

"If you like, although I'm not sure I have the right walking boots for the occasion."

"Nonsense, you have a pair in the wardrobe. I saw you unpack them."

"No, Bill." Julia catches my eye and jerks her head towards her husband. "Back me up, Eliza. Some boots are designed for less treacherous terrains. The Chelsea boots I brought with me are for well-laid paths and shop floors. The boots he needs me to wear are proper walking boots with sturdy soles and proper ankle grip. It makes a huge difference, doesn't it, darling?"

She looks to me for support and just thinking of the trainers I wear everywhere, I brazen it out and nod in agreement. "Yes, it's why there are so many shops selling them. I mean, you wouldn't expect to buy a pair of shopping boots in the outdoor shop, just as you wouldn't find a pair of walking boots in Jimmy Choo."

I know I'm trying a little too hard here because when the hell have I ever opened a door to a Jimmy Choo shop but I need to get Julia on side here and solidarity sisters is definitely something I need to nurture if I'm going to persuade her I'm not after her husband.

Blake is watching me with a slight twist to his lips and I know he has the measure of me. I try to ignore him, but it's increasingly difficult because he is holding my future hostage and I still don't know why.

Bill holds out his hand and Julia walks across, allowing him to pull her in for a sweet hug and once again, it reaffirms my need for a man like Bill in my life. Sweet, caring, considerate, and charming. Nothing like his son. The complete opposite of him and as our eyes connect, I feel the heat spreading through my body like a bush fire. I can't deny the attraction is so hot it burns. He is definitely a catch, but there's something so arrogant about him it rubs me up the wrong way and so I turn my back and fuss with the table instead because I will not play these mind games with him.

They say never turn your back on the enemy and this is why because I'm suddenly aware he's behind me and tucking a stray piece of hair that's fallen from my sloppy ponytail, he announces to the room, "I thought Eliza could show me around today to give you some privacy."

I look up in haste and see his parents smiling as they stand together watching Blake's show.

Bill catches my eye and I try desperately to smile as I say in a false sweet voice, "It would be my pleasure."

More than anything I need Julia to see I have no designs whatsoever on her husband, and she visibly relaxes when she nods her approval. "What a great idea, darling. Eliza will point out all the places of interest, and your father and I can have the run of the place."

Wondering why that's necessary, I'm suddenly conscious of Blake's fingers brushing against mine and I feel like capturing one and bending it backwards just to make a point. I know what he's doing. He's trying to seduce me with his good looks and considerate gestures. Ordinarily, I would be more than happy about that, but there is something about Blake Monroe that gets to me. Maybe it's the arrogant edge he wears so well and the fact he believes he can just click his fingers and I'll come running. He probably thinks I'd be grateful because he's obviously a catch. A good one at that. But I'm just finding Eliza Benson, not a whole heap of heartbreak, so I step away and say breezily, "If you're ready, I'll bring the breakfast in."

Without looking at him, or his parents, I head back to the kitchen, where I wish I could hide all day and barricade myself in.

Dorothy, like the saint she is, has set out bowls of fresh fruit and natural yoghurt, with various nuts and superfood to mix in to their taste. The juice is resting in a crystal glass jug filled with ice and slices of oranges and she whispers, "I have some eggs benedict available, or an omelette. I can do a full English if they prefer, just ask what they'd like."

She hands me the laden tray and I spy another one filled with wheat toast and glass dishes with compote and preserves. It all looks super healthy, but I'm really craving a plate heaped high with bacon, eggs, and sausages right now and to hell with health. I need all the comfort food I can eat because my life will probably end soon, anyway, so I may as well enjoy the small pleasures while I can.

* * *

ONCE AGAIN, I thank God for Mrs Jenkins and by the time the Monroes have finished breakfast, she has tidied up and prepared my full English as ordered, before promising to drop around the evening meal later. She brought lunch with her, and I am eternally grateful and wonder how I can repay her generosity. It's not just her either. It's Sammy Jo too. She has bent over backwards to make this easy for me, which renews my faith that there are kind people out there who require nothing more than to help a person in need. I know I'm a fraud, but my need is great and I'm sure that after a few more days of assistance, I'll be more than able to hold my own in the kitchen. YouTube is a great domesticate bible and I watch endless videos on my phone about cleaning to get ahead. A crash course in domestic bliss that has been rudely interrupted by a man with a hidden agenda.

As soon as Dorothy leaves, I fall on the feast she left me and my heart sinks when I'm caught splashing the ketchup on a big fat sausage by my nemesis Blake.

"Impressive."

"Thank you." I have decided not to engage him in conversation with questions and try to ignore him when he takes the seat next to me and pinches one of my precious slices of bacon.

"Do you mind?"

"No." He grins as he taunts me with his eyes, and I sigh. "Can I help you?"

"I thought that was my department."

"I'm sorry." I shake my head as if he's lost a few brain cells. "I don't speak in riddles. Just tell me what you want from me because I don't buy your good Samaritan act in the slightest."

As he moves to grab a piece of sausage, I consider jabbing my fork into it and as he dips it into ketchup, I'm surprised when he holds it to my lips and says in a slightly sensuous voice, "Allow me."

He makes it feel like a sex act as he pushes the piece of meat inside my mouth and runs his thumb across my lips to wipe the sauce away. Then he licks it off his fingers, causing my body to betray me in the cruellest way.

He affects me, he knows he does, but that doesn't make me like him, so I say tartly, "Have you finished because I would like to enjoy my break in peace?"

He leans back and watches me through those startling eyes. "So, we have the day, well, the morning at least. Where are you going to take me?"

"Do I have a choice?"

"Not really."

I can tell he's enjoying this, so I sigh. "I'll show you the local town. To be honest, it's the only place other than the beach that I know. I haven't been touring the district on a jolly you know. I am here to work."

"So I believe."

"Anyway…" I swallow my mouthful and place my cutlery together. "If you'll excuse me, I'll finish up here and meet you by the front door."

"Ten minutes."

"Fifteen."

He laughs. "Twelve, and if you're late, I get to choose our activity."

"If you like. I couldn't care less what we do because I am being paid to be your babysitter, and it is definitely not my choice, so why would where we go matter to me?"

Without waiting for a reply, I stage sigh heavily and turn my back on him because I may have to spend the morning, if not the next couple of weeks with him, but I don't have to like it.

CHAPTER 18

*T*wenty minutes later, I saunter out and feel a moment's satisfaction that I kept him waiting. He is leaning against Bill's jeep, checking his phone and my heart skips a beat when I stare at most women's idea of perfection. He is wearing black jeans that accentuate his strong, muscled legs. Brown boots and a white t-shirt with a tantalising v at the neck. His brown leather jacket is stylishly battered, and his dark hair is slightly messy on top, creating an urge in me to brush it in place with my fingers. Then he directs those dreamy blue eyes in my direction and pointedly looks at his watch. "You are eight minutes late, which now means you owe me."

Rolling my eyes, I adopt a bored expression, hating the way my heart flutters when he regards me as if he wants to devour me.

"Whatever."

Heading his way, I also hate that I've made more of an effort than I do with Bill. I brushed out my rather ordinary brown hair, wishing I'd had it highlighted before I came. Unusually for me, I attempted to apply my make-up like a professional and pulled on my jeans and a flouncy blue top, grabbing my favourite leather jacket that has definitely seen better days. As always, I'm wearing my trusty trainers, which hopefully gives me the edge if I need to run like the wind if the situation dictates a speedy getaway because I still haven't ruled out murdering him before the day is out.

He holds open the passenger door and says with a low command to his voice, "Get in."

Feeling like a Labrador must, I'm just glad I don't have a tail that would be wagging at him, despite the frown on my face. Why do animals do that? They adore a man or woman who barks commands at them and orders them around, while they offer puppy dog eyes and complete adoration and undeserved loyalty. I am that dog inside, but I would rather die than admit that to him, so with a deep, irritated sigh, I push past him and fumble with my seat belt with a disinterested, "OK, let's get this over with. I have work to do."

He jumps into the driver's seat and says sarcastically, "Of course you do."

As he pulls away, heading towards the road leading to the town, he laughs, making me say irritably, "What's so funny?"

"You."

"Great, I'll add comedian to my curriculum vitae. Thanks for the tip."

"You're welcome. I'm always here for you."

"Well, I wish you weren't."

I'm being rude, but I don't care because I hate how on edge he makes me feel.

"You don't mean that."

"I can assure you I do."

Feeling as if this conversation is going downhill faster than the jeep at the moment, I sigh and force myself to say, "Listen, I'm sorry. I'm not normally this rude, but for some reason you have put me on the defensive."

"I know."

"Anyway…" I ignore his smug answer and try to force some warmth into my voice. "Let's start again. Hi, I'm Eliza Benson. I'm pleased to meet you."

"Do we really have to do this?" He laughs and I say through gritted teeth. "Just humour me."

"OK."

He smirks. "I'm pleased to meet you, Eliza Benson. I'm Blake Monroe, and I feel as if I know you already."

"Is that right?"

He nods and I am trying hard not to stare at his strong capable hands that are gripping the steering wheel with confidence that somehow causes a shiver to pass through every feeling part of my body, which is the whole of it, apparently.

"Yes, I know you are thirty in three weeks' time. You live at home with your parents, which explains a lot."

"Excuse me?"

He chuckles. "You excelled at college and passed your exams with top grades, which helped secure your place at Pemberley Thompson, a leading London solicitor who put you to work in a soulless job that you drag your reluctant feet to five days a week. You are approaching some kind of crisis because you don't know what you want to do with your life, brought on by the unfortunate sounding Annalise Turtle. You want adventures because your life is so boring you can't imagine spending the next thirty years doing the same and you crave excitement. You want to find your soulmate and spend your life together, making the most of it. Riches don't interest you as much as a connection because you are a romantic at heart and are up for most things that give you pleasure. You have yet to work out who Eliza Benson really is and hope that this experience will steer you in a more interesting direction."

"You're wrong."

The fact he's spot on unnerves me a little and he says with an amused, "We both know I'm not."

"Well, part of it is true, but you've just read more into it than there is."

Staring out of the window, I think about his assessment and wonder how he has seen through me in such a short space of time. Bill must have briefed him. That's the only possible explanation and I decide to shift the focus onto him for once and say casually, "If you ask me, you were talking about yourself."

"Is that so?"

"Yes. You see, I know you, Blake Monroe. You still live at home, even though you are obviously way over thirty."

His low chuckle makes me smile as I resort to petty digs to annoy him. "You don't lift a finger and expect your mother to do everything because you're a mummy's boy at heart. You work making money because that inflates your already over-inflated ego and makes you feel as if you're better than everybody else. You're not good with people and think that telling is better than asking and you are overbearing and dominant and don't know anything about reading people."

"I can't deny the facts, but you got the person wrong."

"I hope so, for your sake."

His low laugh makes me smile and a little of the chill goes out of the air as we relax a little.

Feeling a little bolder, I say with genuine interest, "So, are you going to tell me why you made up that strange boyfriend story? It's kind of weird, you know."

"Not to me."

"Then you're weird."

I smirk and stare out at the landscape and relax back against the leather seat. Despite the company, this beats working in London any day of the week and just thinking I may be out of a job if Julia has her way, I say anxiously, "Your mother doesn't really think I'm after your father, does she?"

"The thought did occur to her after your inebriated story about your idol."

"Bill knows, though. I mean, I haven't given him any reason to think I'm anything but the housekeeper he employed."

"He didn't?"

"Didn't what?" I'm confused, and he says with an air of smugness, "He didn't employ you."

"Well, you're wrong because I answered the ad posted by Mr Monroe for a live-in housekeeper, slash assistant, for six months. So, tell me, Mr. I know it all. Why would he employ a young woman in her prime if he thought your mother would be unhappy about that?"

"He didn't employ you. I did."

"But…" I'm speechless and he says as if bored already, "I'll explain when we find somewhere to sit and chat. Maybe there's a pub nearby, or a coffee shop. Although maybe you should steer clear of alcohol in the foreseeable future, it obviously doesn't agree with you."

"It's not the only thing." I can't resist baiting him and, to my surprise, he just laughs out loud. "You know, Eliza…"

"What, I'm dying to know?" I roll my eyes, but then he drops the cocky attitude and says softly, "I knew you'd be perfect, and you are."

For a moment, I don't have words. He has astonished me because that sounded almost genuine. Heartfelt even, with a touch of wistful drizzled on top. It makes me look at him differently because I sense a sadness, yearning even and I don't know how to answer him. Luckily, we arrive in Dream Valley town, and I don't have to because he peers through the windscreen and says, "There's a space outside a shop that must serve drinks at least, judging by the name."

We pull up outside The Cosy Kettle and for the first time since I met him, I'm looking forward to what happens next because there appears to be many layers to Blake Monroe. Inadvertently, he has just revealed there is a human lurking underneath that I am keen to know more about.

CHAPTER 19

The Cosy Kettle is the kind of place you want to tuck yourself in a corner with a good book and waste a day. Warm, welcoming, and stuffed full of cakes and pastries that would make anybody sacrifice their diet in a heartbeat.

It's about half full and we grab a table in the corner and a rather surly looking waitress stops by and says in a bored voice, "What can I get you?"

I share a look with Blake who doesn't look impressed and I'm guessing he could throw a few suggestions her way she wouldn't like, judging by the disapproval on his face.

"Do you have a menu?"

She points to a cardboard one, standing proudly by a lone flower in a jar, and Blake says rather shortly, "Give us a few minutes and we'll let you know."

She doesn't say a word and just turns and leaves and I giggle at the rather dazed expression on his face. "She should really get some training in customer service, that was textbook everything wrong."

"Do you think they have a budget for such things? She's probably the owner's daughter being forced to do something to earn her keep or pocket money."

"She's not that young. She should know better."

Blake shakes his head and grabs the menu and hands it to me, saying, "Choose whatever you like, my treat."

"OK." I smirk as he looks surprised, and I shrug. "You owe me more than a cake and a latte; you owe me an explanation to go with it."

"Possibly." He leans back and regards me with interest as I lean forward and stare him right in the eye. "Possibly?"

He nods. "I don't have to explain myself to you."

Shrugging, I turn my attention to the menu and make him wait in silence until I snap it shut and toss it across the table to him.

"Your turn."

"What are you having?"

"You'll have to wait and see."

I look at my phone, effectively dismissing him and then am mortified when he clicks his fingers at the surly waitress to come over.

"What was that?" I stare at him with a furious look of derision, and he shrugs. "What?"

"That. Clicking your fingers like she's a servant or something. You really are a grade one idiot."

"It got her attention."

As the waitress heads over, looking even more annoyed than before, I hiss, "You had better leave her a big tip after that assholery behaviour."

"That's not even a word."

"I have many 'not even words' for you, Mr Monroe, and I doubt you'd like any of them."

He just laughs as if I've said something hilarious and as the girl reaches us, I'm astonished when he flashes the most bewitching smile, causing her to blink in surprise. Then I watch her transform before my eyes as she visibly relaxes and stands a little taller, before batting her lashes at him and saying coyly, "What can I get you, sir?"

She steps a little closer to his side of the table and tosses her hair back in a provocative way, and if I wasn't seeing this with my own eyes, I would never believe it.

All of this because of one smile. I've got to hand it to him. He's good.

"Ladies first." He points in my direction, and she reluctantly turns her attention to me as I smile warmly. "I would love a half shot, full fat latte and a slice of your delicious looking Victoria sponge please, um…" I wait for her to offer her name and she just looks at me with a bored expression. "Anything else?"

"No thank you…" I encourage a little more and she just looks at me as if I'm the idiot and turns eagerly to Blake, who flashes me an amused grin and regards her through those sparkling blue eyes. "Maybe you could help with that…"

He arches his brow, and she says quickly, "Laura."

Are you freaking serious? I stare in disbelief as she opens up to him and he is trying hard to contain the conceited grin that I know will soon make an appearance.

"Well, Laura, pretty name, by the way." She actually giggles and I sink back in my seat and consider waving the white paper napkin in defeat.

"What do you suggest?"

"Definitely our coffee of the day."

"Sounds interesting. What is it?"

"Gingerbread latte with a side order of ginger cake."

"Perfect." She writes it down and then says slightly breathlessly, "Will there be anything else, sir?"

I'm feeling invisible right now as he leans slightly forward and stares deep into her eyes. "I'll call you if I can think of anything."

She actually blushes and reluctantly moves away, and I hate

the smug look on his face that I am itching to clean off with the flat of my hand.

"Lesson one. Make an impression and play to their weakness."

"Is that what you were doing? I'd call it using sex to score points. Cheap move."

"Sex!" He laughs out loud.

"You were openly flirting with her. You used your eyes in a suggestive way, making her think you were interested. You relied on the fact she stupidly finds you attractive and thought there could be more on offer. You used her to get what you want and will probably walk away and never think of her again while she keeps her eyes trained on that door, waiting for you to return and carry her off like in Officer and a Gentleman."

"You sound as if you know the script already. Maybe you had a similar experience."

"Of course not. I just know people. I study them and can assess a person within seconds of knowing them."

"What if your assessment is wrong?"

"Then I'm still waiting. Why? Am I wrong?"

"Not entirely." He silently claps and then leans forward and stares into my eyes, making me shift awkwardly on my seat. "What about me?"

"What about you?"

"Tell me your assessment of me."

"I already did, or is memory retention a problem for you?"

"Oh, I don't mean your rather inaccurate portrayal of my life, hoping that it mirrors your own unfortunate one. I mean, what do you think my intentions are towards you?"

His words take me back because now it's coming out. The reason for his strange behaviour and the job offer.

"I don't know. I'm still working that out."

"Then you disappoint me."

Leaning back, he stares at me with a thoughtful look, and I shrug. "I don't care if I have. I never set out to impress you, Blake,

113

or should I call you, sir? You seem to like that. It strokes your pompous ego, apparently."

"My pompous ego, interesting." He leans forward and I swear my heart flutters. "I like the stroking part, but I can think of better things to stroke than my ego."

"So can I."

He looks surprised and I grin. "That self-satisfied smile, for one. Not so much a stroke as a punch, but you get the idea."

He actually laughs and smiles at Laura as she heads across with our order.

"That was quick. You're impressive."

She looks so happy I can't deny he has brought a little sunshine to her day and who am I to begrudge her that? Like me, she is stuck in a job she obviously just tolerates, and I wonder what she would rather be doing now. Mind you, the way she is looking at Blake, I think I have my answer and for a moment I leave them to their mutual appreciation society and wonder what's going on. He definitely has an agenda, and I'm hoping that once we scrub out our battle lines, he will tell me what this is all about.

CHAPTER 20

*T*hankfully, Laura leaves and as I take a bite of my sponge, Blake shakes his head. "I never had you down as a vanilla kind of girl."

Why did I cross my legs when he said that? I'm feeling all kinds of crazy right now as I try to maintain a disinterested air. "Then it proves you don't know how to read a person. I like vanilla in just about every aspect of my life, so sorry to disappoint you, Captain Adventure. You obviously formed the wrong opinion about me."

"I doubt that." The rather sexy way he is looking at me is almost unbearable, because Blake Monroe is more than interesting to me. I am loving our banter and the way he undresses me with his eyes. It's not often I feel desirable. Nobody has ever pursued me like this and rather than turning me off, it's turning me on and I'm ashamed of myself.

Struggling to get a grip, I revert to business.

"So, the moment of truth. Why did you give me the job and why does it involve pretending to be your girlfriend?"

"Who said it involved pretending?"

The cake hovers halfway between the plate and my mouth as I stare at him in shock.

Then he winks and says with a laugh, "Relax, I'll tell you everything, although it may sound a little far-fetched."

"Like my life at the moment."

Taking another bite of the cake, I prepare to hear this fanciful story for myself and to my surprise, he sighs heavily and looks a little emotional.

"It's my father."

I don't like the pain that surfaces in his eyes and suddenly I've lost my appetite.

"What about him?"

"He's sick."

I swallow hard because if he is going to tell me something bad about Bill, I need to prepare myself.

Leaning closer, he lowers his voice, causing me to follow his lead and to anyone looking on, it would appear we are whispering sweet nothings in one other's ears.

"He suffered a heart attack a few weeks ago, and it was fifty-fifty if he would survive."

I am speechless and feel an overwhelming urge to grasp his hand in a gesture of support.

Resisting the urge, I say with concern, "But he's ok now."

"Not really."

"What do you mean?"

"He had an operation. It was kept out of the press on his request and the producers agreed to write him out for six months to give him time to recover."

"So, that's why he's here, to recover."

"Among other things."

"Like what?"

"He really is writing that screenplay, and I suppose the heart attack made him look at his future differently. He feels vulnerable, as I'm sure you can imagine, and is questioning where he goes from here."

I know what that feels like and yet I don't have added health complications getting in the way and I stare at Blake with compassion because, from his expression, he is struggling to deal with this.

"So, you advertised for a housekeeper to keep him fed and watered?"

"Sort of."

"What do you mean, sort of?"

Blake sighs and pulls back a little.

"Do you mind if we continue this conversation somewhere more private? I don't feel comfortable talking about my family business in public because if word got out..."

"It's fine. Where do you have in mind?"

"The beach perhaps."

"Ok. Sounds like a plan."

I watch him head to the counter where he flatters Laura some more, and she blushes as if she's on fire, which I know exactly what that feels like. Then he heads back and offers me his hand. "Come on. Let's get some fresh air."

Pretending I don't see his hand and feeling like a bitch for it, I brush past him and bolt for the door because I wanted to grip on so tightly it shocked me. Just a hint of vulnerability in the man has me crumbling, and I must protect my heart at all costs. I won't be swayed by a sob story and a hint of emotion because I need to look after myself first. Something tells me that one bite from the cherry will have me addicted and if I know anything, that's a road leading nowhere.

We head back to the car and the conversation pauses as I direct him to the coast road. Rather than head home to Rock House, we decide to give his parents some alone time and park in the public car park just off Dreamy Sand beach.

By the time we've negotiated the space and purchased a parking ticket, my curiosity is at maximum levels.

Walking with a man like Blake is an experience I'm unlikely to forget. I notice the admiring glances he attracts from the women that pass and even the men check him out. I feel quite inferior to him, which I hate and if anything, it makes me determined to sharpen up my image. I need to power dress down and adopt an effortless chic even when casually dressed. Blake has this perfected, and I wonder if that's what being born into money gives you. A posh chic that tells onlookers you are considerably richer than them.

Blake is quiet and I'm not sure what he's thinking and despite my resistance to him, I find myself wishing my hand was firmly planted in his as we walk side by side on the sand.

The sea is gentle today, the waves gliding in rather than crashing to shore, and even the seagulls are quieter than normal, almost as if they sense an emotional outburst on the horizon.

Blake points towards a cluster of rocks and says, "Shall we sit over there? It may not be that comfortable, but it would be nice to chill for a bit."

"Sure, it's fine."

Those rocks are quite familiar to me because that's where I sat the other day with my book, and it was more comfortable than you might think.

Blake is obviously a true gentleman because he removes his jacket and says with a chivalry I quite like, "Take a seat."

"But your jacket, it will be ruined."

"It's fine. It needs battering a little more. I prefer the worn look."

Trying desperately hard not to focus on his strong muscular arms that have now revealed themselves, I sit on his jacket and shift a little so he can sit beside me. Wondering if this was his plan all along, I push the thought away and try to get my breathing under control as I maintain indifference.

"So…"

He looks out to sea and sighs. "You've met my mother. Well, she is all about appearances and doing things the right way. Well, when they came up with the plan for my father's recuperation, she researched this place. A high standard of accommodation and away from unwelcome visitors. Plenty of sea air and a quiet place for my father to write his screenplay."

"I can agree with that. It was a good choice."

He nods, twisting his hands together as if he needs to keep them occupied.

"Well, she was never going to give up her commitments, as she calls them, to bury herself in the sticks for six weeks. Don't get me wrong, she adores my father, but Julia Monroe is the queen of her court, and she loves every minute of it. So, we needed someone who would be up for the job."

"I get that, but it still doesn't explain this girlfriend thing you keep going on about."

He turns and his twisted grin makes my heart beat a little faster because there's a sense of mischief in his eyes that's infectious.

"That's the part I'm not really that proud of."

"What part?"

"The part where I planned this whole thing just to spend some time with you."

CHAPTER 21

*H*is words roll around my head like a ball in a pinball machine. Spend time with me, but why?

He looks a little sheepish as he says, "Don't get me wrong, the job was exactly as advertised. The thing is mum didn't know anything about the advert."

"Then she must have questions because I know I do."

I'm more than confused, and Blake looks a little guilty.

"I told mum to leave it with me. I had contacts and would find someone who was able to keep a secret. I knew my father would hate being stuck with someone with no personality, so I had quite the job on my hands because most people that apply for positions like this are either slightly weird or have made it their occupation."

"Is that a bad thing? I mean, surely you wanted someone professional, anyway."

"Yes, but we need to keep him here and my father is known for his short attention span and a thirst for life. So, I placed the ad and vetted all the applications. Yours stood out from all the others; despite the fact it was obvious you had no experience."

"It did." My heart sinks because I thought I was being clever about my exaggeration of the truth, and Blake laughs. "It all sounded plausible, but I read between the lines and when I met you it reinforced my judgement."

"But I'd already got the job. You didn't even bother to interview me."

"I did."

"No, you didn't. I think I'd know."

He is talking in riddles and a sly grin transforms his face once more, making me hitch my breath as I wait to hear something I may not like.

"I told you. I narrowed down my choice and then, by chance, found myself in the vicinity of Pemberley Thompson."

"My Pemberley Thompson?"

"Is there any other?" He raises his eyes and I fall silent because this is getting weirder by the second.

"I was in the coffee shop across the road and wondered if you were working that day. Maybe I could head inside and check you out without you knowing. I find you can tell a lot more about a person when they're not on their best behaviour and I was curious."

I'm starting to feel uncomfortable, and he shifts a little, so his leg touches mine and for the first time I don't move away. That surprises me, but not as much as when he says, "As it turns out, I didn't need to because the door opened, and you walked in. I didn't know it was you at first, but then somebody called your name and you answered. Your name is quite unusual, so I was sure it was my Eliza Benson who had answered the ad."

Now I'm feeling even more worried, and he appears quite pleased with himself when he laughs. "It was quite the conversation I overheard."

"You were spying on me."

This time, I do move my leg away and glare at him as he smiles apologetically.

"I suppose I was. Apparently, you were telling your friend all about a disastrous date you had the night before. It made for entertaining listening, and I believe your words were, *if only I could meet a real man. Someone who would just take charge, like in those trashy books I read when I'm pretending to read War and Peace on the tube."*

I look down, wishing the sea would just roll on in and carry me away.

"Mind you…" he carries on, "The guy sounded like a loser. You were well rid of him, anyway."

My face burns because the guy he is referring to is a man who I never want to see again. Geoffrey Armitage, a trainee accountant who spent the whole date recording every purchase in an app on his phone. He grilled me about my investments and told me I should be putting money into an Isa and what was my pension fund sitting at currently? I was in Dullsville, and he even said at the end of the night that if I wanted to go home with him and have sex, he had an hour before his mother came home from bingo.

Blake laughs out loud. "If I remember rightly, you said you were looking for the romantic adventure. A Christian Grey to your Ana, a Shaggy to your Scooby Doo, and a Danny to your Sandy. You wanted to lurch from adventure to adventure and drag your soulmate along for the ride. You were done with internet dating and needed a real man, not a side swipe. You even threatened to join the army but decided khaki just wasn't your colour and you were seriously contemplating joining a circus somewhere because your mum would never live down the embarrassment at her country club."

"I get the picture." I groan and place my head in my hands. "The question is, why did you hire me? I wouldn't."

"Because you were perfect."

Chancing a look in his direction, I see him looking at me with a strangely tender look and I swallow hard and whisper, "For what?"

"For being my girlfriend."

I break the stare and say slightly hysterically, "Please, can you stop? If anything, I should be karate chopping you right now and reporting you to the stalker police."

"Then let me explain myself."

"Finally." I say with relief, and he leans back against the rock and smiles.

"As I said, mum wouldn't trust a stranger, so I told her I had a friend who was in between jobs right now."

"You lied to her." He nods. "And I continue to because don't get me wrong, if my mother really thought you were a house-keeper, you wouldn't have passed the application process. This way, she was safe in the knowledge you would keep my father's health problems within the family and the only interest you have in him is as a potential father-in-law."

I feel a little faint at the thought, and he grins. "You see, my mother is overly protective of my father, and especially his public image. The last thing she wants is word getting out he's in ill health. She thinks it would cause the public to write him off and tarnish his daytime crown. She would be the subject of gossip and her so-called friends would pity her. This way, she saves face by telling her 'friends' that he's working on a screenplay, which by the time she finishes, will be in line for a Bafta next year. She has the loyalty of a housekeeper who will protect their secret and not think of hitting on her husband. It was the only way and our visit this weekend was to reassure her that everything was in place and to give me time with you."

"She thinks I'm your girlfriend. What happened to a friend?"

"I may have told her we were more than that." He says sheep-ishly and I say in a puzzled voice, "But why?"

"Because I'm fed up with her trying to set me up with her friend's daughters. It's an endless attack and I'm weary of it."

"So, you're using me." I should be annoyed about that, but for some reason it makes me feel a lot better. Suddenly, I don't see him as a weird stalker and just a practical businessman who saw a way to deal with all his troubles in one go. If anything, I'm impressed, and I breathe a sigh of relief.

"So, what happens now?"

"We carry on as before with the added complication that I'm staying for a couple of weeks."

"So you said. Why is that?"

"I have business here, believe it or not, and it's also a good place to concentrate on my own project. I've been told to work from home until it's complete and I thought I'd take care of the other side of things and keep an eye on my father at the same time. Mum is happy, although after your story about the gold digger, she was worried you would transfer your attention to her husband but now she can head back to Wimbledon and announce the screenplay is doing well and I'm holidaying with a love interest."

His piercing blue eyes cut through me and suddenly I'm struggling to breathe. We are so close together on this rock, even a stiff breeze could push us together and I find myself wishing that it would. Now I know he's not a psychopath, just a very conniving businessman bent on self-preservation, I like him even more.

As the wind whips around my hair, I'm taken aback when he reaches out and tucks it behind my ear and as he gazes into my eyes, he says huskily, "So, are you up for the challenge?"

"Which is?"

"Pretending to be my girlfriend, of course."

"But I wouldn't actually have to do anything, would I?"

I'm hating that I'm hoping he tells me otherwise, and he shakes his head slowly. "No, of course not. Dad thinks you're the hired help and mum thinks you're my secret girlfriend. Both are happy about that, and I get my mother off my back with her endless match making. I enjoy a break for two weeks in interesting company and at the end of it, we all go our separate ways and live our best lives."

I feel so relieved because now it's all crystal clear. Blake knows I'm not Mary Poppins, so I no longer need to impress him. Bill is happy, and I get to learn new skills in a glorious setting. The only person who I need to be careful around is Julia because she thinks I'm Blake's girlfriend and may mention that. The fact she's heading home tonight means I can relax, and if she needs confirmation, I'm happy to oblige.

CHAPTER 22

We spend the next hour discussing how to play this and I must admit it's been a while since I had so much fun. Blake can be quite charming when he wants to be and is an easy companion to talk to. He told me about his job and how much he loves it. He works in the city and never really felt the need to get his own place when his family home was a short tube ride away. After our brief chat I've realised he likes to make money but doesn't believe in wasting it and I must admire that about him.

As we start to head back, he says a little tentatively, "So, are you ok about this?"

"I suppose so. I mean, some girls would be flattered, I suppose."

"Some girls that don't include you." A smile tugs at the corner of his mouth, and I grin. "Correct."

"So, what does Eliza Benson look for in a potential partner?"

"Let me see." I pretend to think and say casually, "He's got to be funny."

"So, you like a comedian then?"

"Who doesn't? It's good to laugh. It cleanses the soul."

"If you say so." He rolls his eyes and I nudge him playfully. "He needs to be normal and let me tell you that's a big ask these days, especially on the dating apps I've tried. I mean, seriously, what is it with the guys on there? They tell you one thing and then when you meet, they are completely different from their profile. Really, there should be rules against stringing a girl along. I am seriously debating whether to join a sailing club instead."

"Do you sail?"

"Not unless you count taking the ferry to France on the odd occasion, but my mum told me that was where the movers and shakers hang out, her words not mine. I mean, what does that even mean? I have this weird image of possible love interests moving around at speed while shaking. It's not a good look at all."

I sigh heavily and Blake laughs out loud. "You're a funny girl, Eliza, you make me laugh."

"Yes, you said I can add comedian to my CV."

He nods. "I'll even give you a reference."

We carry on walking, and I think back on his question. What do I look for in a man? I suppose I've never thought that hard about it before, but now he's asked, I feel like a fool for not outlining my goals in that department. Feeling curious, I ask, "What do you look for in a woman, other than she's breathing, of course?"

I nudge him playfully and he nudges me back, which feels kind of nice. I'm enjoying the fact we're getting along now, and I suppose it's because I know where I stand and don't feel on edge around him.

"Funny, obviously."

"Of course, the number one reason."

He nods and starts ticking off the list on his fingers. "Good conversation, not self-obsessed, and always looking for the next best thing. Able to enjoy roughing it a bit by camping or hiking. Sailing obviously…" he winks, making me giggle and he pretends to think hard. "Somebody with ambition perhaps and not content to stay in one place all her life. A friend and a lover, of course."

Suddenly, I'm feeling very hot and wonder if the mercury levels have increased since this morning, but I know it's got absolutely nothing to do with the temperature and everything to do with him. A lover. A man like that. I could only imagine what that would be like and the fact he's telling me his idea of the perfect woman makes me want to take notes and study for the part. I don't meet many men like Blake Monroe. Quite honestly, I don't think I ever have and now he's here and attached to me in a roundabout way, my mind is racing with the possibilities. Could he fall in love with me? Is that even an option?

"Hey, you've gone quiet on me."

Once again, he nudges me and I say slightly wistfully, "Do you think our perfect partner is out there? I mean, how would you even know? It's not as if the opposite sex comes with an instruction manual."

"I think attraction plays a part and personality turns that attraction into love."

"Where did you read that?" I try to lighten the atmosphere and I'm surprised when he stops and pulls me around to face him and the look in his eye makes me stop and stare.

"I think you know almost immediately."

"You do?"

He leans a little closer and if anyone was looking, they would take a picture and caption it 'romance novel' because the waves are sparkling in the crystal sea behind us, and the sun is beating down, casting us in its radiant glow.

This is the moment in the movie when happily ever after makes an appearance and as Blake leans closer, I feel my heart racing because I want him to kiss me more than I've ever wanted anything.

"Stay still."

I am frozen to the spot as he lifts his hand towards my face, and I tremble inside. Then he brushes his fingers against my temple and says softly, "Some say it's lucky."

"What is?" My voice is hitched and his eyes twinkle as he drops his hand and removes a tissue from his pocket.

"Bird poo."

"Excuse me."

"A seagull just made a deposit on your head. You may want to wash your hair when we get back."

My hand flies to my hair and Blake laughs as he hands me the tissue. "It's all I've got. I'm sorry, maybe it's a sign we should head back."

The spell has been machined gunned into non-existence and, feeling self-conscious, I try to laugh it off. "Lucky me."

His low chuckle makes me feel like a fool because I really thought we had a moment back there. Maybe he doesn't feel it; perhaps this is all in my imagination, but just for a second, I found my soulmate. At least it certainly felt that way.

CHAPTER 23

*J*ulia meets us looking as if she's been modelling for Cosmopolitan. Her silk kimono flutters in the breeze coming from the bifold doors, where she is standing gazing out at the picture postcard view, while sipping what appears to be a large gin and tonic.

Blake says with some surprise, "Should you be drinking? I thought you were heading home tonight."

"Tomorrow, darling. I have extended my stay for a few hours because tennis was cancelled due to the coach missing his flight back from Puerto Rico."

She smiles happily. "So, a window of opportunity presented itself and I informed your father he had the pleasure of my company for another night."

Blake nods, seemingly unconcerned, and Julia steps forward and holds out her hand.

"Give me your jacket, darling, and I'll hang it up for you."

"Sure."

I watch in amazement as he shrugs out of it, and she screws up her nose. "This is marked, darling, scuffed even. What one earth have you been…"

Her gaze flicks to me and I know she is looking at my unruly hair that I have scrubbed with the tissue and coupled with the wind from the beach, my face is flushed and my eyes bright. With a sinking feeling, I know how this looks as she smirks and whispers, "You may want to clean up, Eliza, darling. We don't want Bill to suspect anything."

My cheeks are now on fire as Blake smirks beside me and I say in a rush, "Of course, um, I won't be long."

As I race from the room, I feel so embarrassed. Then again, if we were together, I'm guessing we would have been doing even more and, once again, my heart flutters when I think of that. I'm pretty certain it would be amazing because from what I've seen, Blake is a man who doesn't do anything by halves and like my perfect fantasy that he so strangely overheard, he is exactly the kind of man I would choose if I could only find the shop that sells them.

* * *

I AM SO grateful for my own personal space in this house. My room is my sanctuary and as I shower away my embarrassment and try to regain control of my heart, I relish some time alone. However, the gods are against me because my mum decides to check in via Facetime, making it doubly worse.

"Hey, Mum."

"Darling, I haven't interrupted anything, have I?"

Her eyes are glancing around the room, and I realise I'm sitting with just a towel wrapped around my hair and one around my body.

"Of course not."

I feel a little irritated at that and she looks confused. "Then why are you showering in the middle of the day?"

"Because I took a walk, and a seagull used me to dump on."

She just laughs out loud, which is one strike against motherly love, and as she wipes her eyes, she says quickly, "So tell me about Bill. I'm still waiting for some photographs. Has he asked about me and just for information purposes, I need two days' notice to travel?"

"Of course he hasn't. Actually, we've been too busy to talk much at all."

"Why?"

Her eyes are wide, and I sigh heavily. "His wife and son arrived yesterday for the weekend but are extending their stay. There's a lot to do with the extra bodies here, like washing, cooking, cleaning etc, etc, etc."

The fact she's laughing makes me frown and as she wipes a tear from her eye, she says, "You know, I am one proud mother right now. Look at you, keeping house and making such a good job of it. I really thought after a few hours they would have politely thanked you for the trial and called in the professionals."

"Thanks for the vote of confidence. Actually, they are very pleased with my work, I'll have you know."

The door slams behind her and she leans closer to the camera on the phone and whispers, "Sorry about this, but your dad read your love letters."

"He did what?" I am so shocked I just stare at the phone because what the hell is good about that statement?

Mum shakes her head and purses her lips, which she always does when she's angry.

"Yes, I came home from aqua aerobics, and he was sitting on the settee having a right good laugh. I asked him what he was reading, and he told me they were from some guy called Richard."

"Richard?" I'm surprised because I don't even know a Richard and she looks a little confused. "He told me dick was mentioned. A lot. I don't think I knew him. Where did you meet him?"

"Mum, please, stop. Those letters were in my wardrobe in a box behind my snow boots. How on earth have they fallen into dad's hands and why does he think it's ok to snoop through my personal stuff?"

For some reason, she looks a little guilty and then mumbles, "Well, because you're away for a while, we decided your room could use a lick of paint, so we emptied it. Obviously, we had to empty the cupboards and drawers to move them, and most of it is in the living room and the larger items on the landing. Your father was taking a break and knocked the box onto the floor and as he was gathering up the letters, one of them fell before his eyes."

"You mean another word for snooping. Honestly mum, letters don't just fall before people's eyes, they are folded in envelopes, and I knew I should have burned those the moment he finished with me for Abigail Lyons."

"What, the girl with bleached blonde hair who dresses like a stripper?"

"Yes."

Mum shakes her head, looking annoyed. "Typical man. They are attracted to porn in every aspect of life. You had a lucky escape there."

She leans a little closer and whispers, "He was surprised at some of the things he read, though. He told me he never knew you were, well, like that."

"Like what?" She opens her mouth to speak, and I say quickly. "Never mind. I don't want to ever talk about this again. Erase it from your memory and tell dad to do the same. If you ever see me again, pretend it was a bad dream because I will absolutely not discuss any aspect of those letters with my probing parents."

"Funny you should use that word. He told me about the part when…"

"Mum, please, I've got to go, and I repeat, never speak of this again and please just shred those letters and then burn what's left."

"Ok love, if you insist. Anyway, I'm free next weekend if you need a visitor. I can bring my sleeping bag if there aren't enough beds."

"No visitors. Goodbye."

I cut the call for my own sanity and stare at the blank screen in disbelief. My father read my love letters. I still can't get over that and the fact they were X-rated is almost causing my heart to fail. Then I think of Bill and his own failing heart and feel bad for agonising over something that's really not important in the grand scheme of things. All it does is remind me I'm very unlucky at love and I should really explore foreign travel and leave the country for a few years until they forget all about my X-rated ramblings.

Blaming puberty, I decide to dress like a Victorian matron and pull a high-necked sweater over my jeans, and finger dry my hair into some kind of style.

By the time I head to the kitchen, I have decided to push aside my disasters and concentrate on being the best housekeeper in the history of domestic service.

CHAPTER 24

Somehow, I manage to heat up the pasta bake that Dorothy prepared and as I pull it from the oven, Julia wanders into the room like a floating mirage. Her kimono billowing behind her, making her look like an exotic bird of paradise.

"That smells divine, darling."

She sits gingerly on the edge of the bar stool and watches me with inquisitive eyes. Feeling like the poor relation, I can tell she is assessing me like any mother of boys would and I expect she sees me as an enemy now, which doesn't make me feel any better about my day.

"How's it going?"

Her soft voice reaches me and as I look up, she winks. "Blake told me about your um, friendship and as his mother, I have many questions, of course."

"You do?" Now I'm afraid because she has the look of a mama bear waiting to pounce if I say anything bad about her baby.

"So, is it going well?"

"I think so."

"Darling," she rolls her eyes. "Don't *think* in life–*know*. I mean, don't second guess anything, just ask. You must know if things are going well because you are fifty percent of the relationship."

"I guess."

She looks a little pensive. "I've been waiting for Blake to show any interest in women."

That's got my attention, and I wonder if there's something he's not telling me.

Julia grins and whispers, "He was a terrible rogue at college. So many girls used to call around unexpectedly, hoping to catch him in."

"They did?"

"Yes. It was just lucky we have electric gates and a door entry system, otherwise I wouldn't get anything done. The trouble is, he's never shown any interest in one particular girl before. It's always been work, work, work."

She stops and fans her face, making me think she's about to faint or something and she gasps, "I'm a little dry, darling. I don't suppose you have any gin lying around?"

Wondering if she has a drink problem, I nod and retrieve it from under the sink where I've hidden it and she sighs with relief. "I hate drinking around Bill at the moment because he's exempt."

"Exempt."

"From drinking?"

I'm not sure if that's the right word to use but think better of correcting her as she seizes the ice-filled glass with eager hands. "I expect Blake told you about his…" she lowers her voice. "condition and alcohol is on the prohibited list, along with sugar, fat and anything fried. It's exhausting keeping him healthy because he is a man who loves to overindulge in every way."

She looks thoughtful. "I suppose we all do in our way. Mine is a healthier indulgence, unless you count the gin. I like fitness and spa breaks. Good nutritious food washed down with the finest champagne. It's my one pleasure and I work hard to enjoy it. I mean, those charity committees and endless public appearances really take it out of me and don't get me started on Blake. He requires a full-time servant; he can do nothing for himself. What can I say? He's still my little boy and always will be."

Thinking about the man who cooked and cared for me yesterday doesn't seem as if she's talking about the same person and I wonder if Julia is the problem here.

Looking behind her, she turns and whispers, "I'm taking Bill out for supper to that lovely Italian restaurant he told me about."

"The Olive Tree."

"That's the one. It will be good to be seen together in public."

"Why?" I'm confused and wonder if I've missed something.

"We don't want any rumours getting out about his ill health. We must protect the brand at all costs and a few pics of me enjoying a date night with my husband on my Instagram feed will keep the vultures at bay."

She sniffs appreciatively and says loudly, "But not until we have sampled that amazing pasta bake. Please make sure Bill only gets a small portion and definitely no wine for him. A glass of filtered water with a slice of lemon should help with his digestion and clean out those inner parts that are otherwise unreachable. Mind you, the enamel on his teeth won't thank me, but there's nothing I can do about that."

She stands and pushes the now empty glass towards me. "A glass of chilled champagne with my lunch should wash that gin and tonic down nicely. Just make sure you tell Bill it's sparkling elderflower. He hates that, so won't want to share mine."

As she flounces off, I wonder about Julia Monroe. Everything is about appearances with her, and I wonder how much is done because of that and not out of concern for Bill. They seem happy enough and it's obvious he idolises her, but there's a nagging doubt that just won't go away. Are they just pretending everything is fine, or are they just papering over the cracks?

* * *

As I serve up the pasta and fill their glasses, I'm surprised when Bill says sweetly, "Come and join us, Eliza, don't sit on your own in the kitchen."

I look at Julia for her reaction and she just looks at Bill fondly and nods, "Of course, it will be lovely, just the four of us."

"I don't miss the wink she gives Blake who, to his credit, just looks back with a bored expression.

Wishing I could escape and eat on my own, I resign myself to a family lunch with people who weave lies into their conversation with practised ease.

"You know, Eliza is a great find because her meals are second to none." Bill tucks into the bowl of pasta and as I catch Blake's eye, his smirk irritates me.

"Thank you." I don't know what else to say and Julia nods in agreement. "Yes, this is delicious. You really should give me the recipe. I mean, is this goat's cheese, or brie? I can't tell."

Blake grins and says loudly, "Yes, please tell us, Eliza, I would love to know too."

"Goats cheese." I don't miss a beat and just smile as if I know the secrets of the Holy Grail.

"Did you use Rigatoni or penne? I'm never sure of the difference?" Julia stares at her bowl as if the answer is written on the side.

"Rigatoni." Once again, I make it up as I go along, and Bill looks confused. "I thought it was penne. Shows what I know."

Blake nods. "Maybe it's a cross breed."

"For goodness' sake, Blake, don't be facetious."

Julia smiles her apology. "Ignore these heathens, Eliza. They wouldn't know spaghetti from capellini."

I raise my eyes, making her laugh and then feel a sharp kick on my ankle.

NEW BEGINNINGS IN DREAM VALLEY

To his credit, Blake is sipping his water and looking unconcerned and in retaliation, I kick him hard in return.

Feeling as if I won that, I'm horrified when Bill grunts in apparent pain and Julia says with alarm, "What's the matter darling? Is it your heart? Do we need to do CPR?"

He rubs his leg, and the realisation hits me, I kicked the wrong leg. Feeling flustered, I reach for the water jug and say quickly, "Please, drink some water. It could help."

His amused grin makes me blush because what have I done? I kicked Bill, which could have turned into another scene from Kill Bill because who thinks it's ok to kick a sick man?

Once Bill assures everyone it was just cramp, we carry on eating, and I feel really bad. To his credit, Bill just throws me reassuring looks, but I still can't believe that happened.

Julia is unconcerned and regales us with tales of the Wimbledon elite and has some rather shocking tales of what goes on during Wimbledon week that I can't wait to share with my mum.

Finally, when I'm excused, I clear the plates away while Julia and Bill head upstairs for a siesta. Maybe that's what happens when you're older and I am looking forward to the part of my life when sleeping during the day is socially acceptable.

CHAPTER 25

*B*lake helps me tidy away and to be honest, I'm glad of it. I think I have mental exhaustion because I'm scared to speak half the time.

"Good kick, by the way." Blake laughs out loud, and I say anxiously, "I feel so bad."

"It was funny, though."

"No, it wasn't. Your poor dad he must wonder what's going on."

"The fact he was playing footsie all through lunch with my mother serves him right."

"They were." I'm stunned and Blake laughs. "Why do you think they've gone for a siesta?"

"Because that's what you do in your fifties, perhaps?"

"I certainly hope not. I can think of more interesting things to do in bed than sleep."

"You mean…"

"I mean nothing."

Turning away, he flicks on the kettle. "Fancy a cup of tea."

"Sure." As I load the dishwasher, I am trying hard to shake the image Blake has deposited in my mind, and I'm not sure I can look them in the face when they return. Blake must be wrong, surely.

Once the tea is made and the dishes cleared, Blake nods towards the garden. "Fancy taking this outside."

"Sure."

I follow him and as I sit on the comfy outdoor furniture, I'm surprised when he squeezes into the seat beside me.

It must show because he says quickly, "It's the best view in the house, so don't read too much into it."

"I wasn't."

"Yes, you were. You think I'm going to pounce."

"No, I don't."

"I can see it in your eyes."

"Do you see how much you annoy me too? Because I'm guessing that's pretty evident in them right now."

His only reply is to stretch his arm lazily along the back of the chair and raise his eyes in a challenge.

"Is this ok?"

"It doesn't bother me."

I try so hard to look unaffected when I am living my best life right now. It almost feels intimate, as if we're really dating and then I'm even more surprised when Blake picks up his phone and says, "Let's take a selfie to mark the occasion."

He snaps away, while my smile is frozen in place. Wishing I could request an AirDrop and post it on my Instagram feed, I act unconcerned and lean forward to grab my tea.

"So, you say you have business here. May I ask what it is, or is it top secret like most things in your family?"

"No, you may ask."

"Thank you, kind sir."

I roll my eyes and he drags out a smile. "There's a new development heading to town called Dream Valley Heights."

"I've heard of that." I look at him in surprise.

"How?" I can tell I have his attention and I remember a conversation I had with Sammy Jo over our drinks.

"My friend's husband is the developer. Marcus Hudson. He inherited the land by all accounts and is keen to develop more of a community in Dream Valley. It sounds amazing, but what's your interest in it?"

"An opportunity."

He looks out to sea and says with a hint of pride in his voice. "I've done well for myself and need a new challenge. I'm happy with where I am, but had the idea of investing some of my earnings into property. It's the only thing that never seems to fail and so I thought about buying two or three houses and renting them out. Once I have them in place, I would buy a few more and sink my money into bricks and mortar the old-fashioned way."

"I don't think of you as old-fashioned, Blake."

He looks anything but and then, to my surprise, he suddenly looks serious.

"I am where it concerns money. It's hard to earn and easy to spend. I want security for my future and my family. So, when I earn a huge bonus for making someone richer than they thought possible, I'm using it to help others."

"More like yourself."

"Not really. You see, I want to rent them out to good honest people who could use a break. Equip them with the luxuries as standard and charge a slightly less than market rent. That way, I hope to attract loyal tenants who will care for my investment."

"That's so nice." I am a little taken aback by this because I thought he was only interested in the bottom line, not people.

"I can be."

"If you say so."

For a moment, the silence sits between us, but it's not awkward and if anything, it feels nice. Surprisingly, the more time I spend with him, the more I like him. He's not as arrogant as I first thought, and we have the same sense of humour and it appears we enjoy similar things. I also like the way he looks after his family's interests and tries to do the right thing by them. Not to mention how gorgeous he is and single handedly the most handsome man I have ever met.

"I have a meeting with him tomorrow." Blake says after a while.

"Marcus?"

"Yes. We're meeting to go over the details."

"I didn't think they'd started building yet."

From my conversation with Sammy Jo, I was under the impression they were still at the planning stage.

"They haven't, but it's the perfect time to work out the details."

"Which are?" I'm curious and don't care if I'm prying, and he says with a hint of excitement, "I want to be in on the start. It's good to build a solid business relationship, and it helps both ways. The development will haemorrhage money and Marcus will need some solid investors to bring on board. If I'm the first in line, I get the best choice which is why I was keen to stay. To cement our relationship and set in place the way forward as business partners."

"It sounds scary. Rather you than me."

A low moan carries along the breeze towards us, and I look at him in surprise. "What was that?"

He raises his eyes to the room just above us where the balcony looks out to sea. "Maybe my mother is having a bad dream."

My cheeks burn as another one follows it and I whisper, "She must be having a nightmare."

I can't resist giggling and Blake nods, the mischief dancing in his eyes. "Obviously."

Another groan follows it and I stare at him with acute embarrassment — for him and he laughs and grabs my hand, pulling me to my feet.

"Where are we going?"

"Anywhere else." The pained look he shoots me makes me giggle and as we set off down the steps, we make our way to the beach below.

It's only when we're away from the house that I notice my hand is still firmly clinging onto Blake's and yet he doesn't seem to notice, or care. It's as if we're really a couple, taking a gentle stroll after lunch and I love how it feels. For a moment I let my imagination run riot and even imagine Rock House is ours. We are in a relationship, marriage even with two children running on the sand in front of us. Blake would be the most amazing father and enjoy playing with his kids, while I would be a caring mother who kept them all safe and happy with my developing domestic skills. Then, when they are tucked up in bed for the night, Blake and I would—"

"What are you thinking?"

"How nice this is." I'm glad he can't see my real thoughts because I'm sure that would amuse him, especially after our rather frosty beginning, and he laughs out loud. "Does this mean I've won you over at last?"

"What do you mean?" I'm confused, and he stops, spinning me around to face him and I groan, "Not again!"

I stare at him with a pained expression, and he looks confused.

"What do you mean, not again?"

"Bird poo, because if it is…"

To my surprise, he looks serious and stares deep into my eyes and says huskily, "No, I stopped you because I wanted to do this."

Two hands reach up and cup my face gently and then soft lips reach out to mine and as they connect, a million fantasises explode into one big moment of destiny as Blake kisses Eliza on the beach in what feels like paradise. The gentle breeze dances around us with glee and the seagulls cry out in celebration. The sun casts its magical glow around us, and life doesn't get any better than this. As he deepens the kiss, I lean into him because this is the single best moment of my life and as he drops his hands and his arms fold around my body, he pulls me close, and we share a kiss that feels as if it's been a long time coming.

CHAPTER 26

*T*here was no embarrassment when the kiss finally ended. If anything, it felt as if we had always been together. We just walked along the sand and talked. About our past, our present and our future. Discovering shared interests and common goals. Blake is an easy companion and I feel no need to keep my guard in place and when we return to Rock House, it's with a different relationship than we had before.

Bill and Julia are lying on the sun loungers by the hot tub, and it feels a little awkward facing them now, but Blake doesn't appear to care and drops into the seat beside his mother as I say quickly, "I'll go and fix some drinks."

Julia yawns loudly. "Super, darling, I could use an energy shot, maybe a smoothie filled with spinach and mango. Do we have those ingredients?"

"I'm not sure we do." I feel like a failure already and Julia says, "I'll help you. Maybe we can rustle one up with what we have. It's so energising, sipping a cocktail while allowing nature to restore your energy levels with sunshine and fresh sea air."

She heaves herself off the lounger and leaving the men to talk, we head inside, and I hope we have some of the ingredients she needs otherwise that will be another strike against my name.

"I could get used to this." Julia sighs. "It's so peaceful here. Nothing like life in Wimbledon where it's all traffic noise and to do lists."

"I agree. Life in London is fast-paced and nothing like this."

"Blake tells me you work in London but are currently reassessing your goals. I must say that was very fortunate for us; it really helped us out of a hole."

"I'm the one who's grateful. It came at just the right time for me too."

She looks thoughtful. "Yes, I remember your story about that woman who made you look at things differently."

Rushing to reassure her that I am nothing like Annalise, I say quickly, "It was just an example, really. I wouldn't want to be like her. I just admired her zest for life."

Julia holds up her hand. "You don't have to make excuses for a lightbulb moment, no matter where it came from. We've all had those in our time, but it takes a courageous woman to act on them. So, tell me, where did you meet Blake?"

Now I'm in trouble because I don't know what he told her, and we didn't think to agree on our cover story. "Oh, I think we've known each other for ages, you know, friends of friends."

She nods and is temporarily distracted by peering into the fridge and I try to steer her away from the topic.

"I'll see if there's a blender."

Quickly, I open the cupboards and I sigh with relief when I see one lurking inside, and as I set it on the counter, she starts pulling fresh vegetables and fruit from the drawers in the fridge.

"Spinach, ah perfect, a little lemon juice is always good. Apple, baby kale, leaves, banana, do we have any frozen pineapple or mango?" I shake my head and she looks thoughtful. "Ice cubes then. That would work and possibly some of this melon, and then all we need is water."

I'm happy to leave her to agree the ingredients because I'm just a little concerned about how the blender works. Surely there's an instruction manual around here somewhere?

"So, tell me, Eliza, what are your plans for the future?"

Her innocent question is anything but because I know what this is – a job interview of sorts that involves a future with her only son.

"I'm just looking at possibilities. I have no clear direction I'm heading in."

She looks up sharply and I say quickly, "I'm trained as a legal secretary and always thought I should improve on that. Maybe take a year off to get this need for adventure out of my system and then study to qualify as a solicitor."

"What a super plan, darling. I wholeheartedly agree with that. You know, so many women have marriage as their main ambition. To live off the hard-earned money of their husband and spend their days frittering it away on material possessions and lunches. Take me, for instance."

I'm wondering what she's about to say because I think she just described herself and she looks almost pensive as she revisits a memory. "I was a young aspiring model when I met Bill. He was already acting in small plays and even a few commercials. We met on the set of an advert for fungal cream. You know the sort; Athlete's foot can be a bugger to get rid of."

She winks and I try so hard to stop giggling at her choice of words, which don't really fit the image, not to mention the thought of them advertising something so gross.

"Well, needless to say, Bill portrayed the athlete. He always did have an athletic body to match his personality, and I was the woman he was trying to impress. I was a mirage of youthful attraction in his dreams and the infection was preventing him from joining me in his make-believe hot tub.

She laughs and rolls her eyes. "Adverts are so ridiculous, aren't they?"

"I think it sounds romantic, if you forget the fungal infection side of it, of course."

She nods, apparently lost in the past. "Well, we got talking and Bill was so charming; he is rather good at that."

I nod in agreement because I have witnessed that side of him first hand and she smiles as she thinks back on how they met.

"We started dating. I would have been a fool not to. He consumed me, Eliza. He took over my life and I couldn't function unless I was thinking of him in some way. I was completely smitten and any ambitions I had were cast aside for love."

"It sounds so romantic."

I am carried along by her story and the love in her eyes, and then she sighs heavily. "I stopped going for castings if they interfered with plans we'd made. I didn't even attempt to go for the major campaigns because they usually involved foreign travel and I couldn't bear to be away from him for a second. I was so worried, you see; Bill's star was rising, and he was attracting attention. I was on edge the whole time, thinking he would be stolen from me. I became a little needy, and it started to drive a wedge between us."

"What happened?" I am holding onto her every word, and she grins ruefully. "We broke up."

"Oh."

I'm shocked because that wasn't what I expected at all, and she stares at me with a hard expression. "You see, darling, there is nothing more off-putting than a woman who is available, always there and monopolising your time. Bill didn't need the added complication of a clinging woman; he was taking every opportunity he had to make it big. I should have done the same. Allowed my own star to rise alongside his. Be more interesting and have conversation when we met up at the end of the day. All I offered him was desperate demands for reassurance that he loved me and promises that he would never leave me. Who wants that, so he cut all ties and started dating a string of beauties to get over me?"

"I'm so sorry. That must have been hard."

"I was destroyed. I had lost everything because I allowed him to become my world. I tried to get back into my own business, but I was yesterday's news already. I had taken my eye off the ball, and it had bounced away to a different corner."

"What did you do?"

"I started over and made it my mission to try again. I went for every casting going, no matter how small, and soon began to edge my way back up the ladder. I tried not to think of anything, but my career and it taught me a very valuable lesson – to always put myself first. Don't rely on anyone else for your own path in life because people have a habit of straying from that path, and some never come back."

"But Bill did." I know there was a happy ending which I am keen to hear more about and Julia nods with a beautiful smile.

"It was a few years later. I'd got over him by then and had even dated a few other men, none of whom ever came close to him, of course. It was while I was on a date, I met him at a film premiere. He was with a popular soap actress, and they were the golden couple in every magazine, newspaper and gossip column. I was with a leading photographer who was quite frankly a total bore and when I met Bill at the after party, it was as if we had never parted."

She grins and I love the sparkle in her eye. "We spent the whole evening dodging our dates and enjoying stolen kisses in the shadows. Bill was on a mission and told me he'd always regretted letting me go. He had watched my career go from strength to strength and was so proud of my journey. By now he was a household name and that worried me because what if history repeated itself? I had come so far and was afraid I'd fall hard, but we were different people then and our relationship strengthened because of the lessons we had learned."

Fixing me with a stern look, she says firmly, "Don't make my mistakes, Eliza. Enjoy your time with Blake, but know his star is rising fast. It may not be in the public eye, but it's every bit as bright. He will be focusing on that, and you may not get the attention you desire. Don't sacrifice your own future for him; be better than me and prove that women are equal and can have it all. He will think more of you because of it and after all, behind every strong man is an even stronger woman, and I should know. I am the machine behind Bill Monroe, and that's why I'm heading back to Wimbledon. To keep the machine going while one of its cogs is under repair. I would love to stay and enjoy some time with my husband, but his star isn't diminishing anytime soon, not all the time he enjoys shining so much."

Thinking of Bill enjoying the attention of his devoted public, the pleasure in his eyes when they clamoured for his attention and the charm he bestowed on them, tells me she's right. The slightly sad look in his eye when he thinks nobody's looking must be because of the illness that's threatening to wake him from the dream. Julia has now shot up in my estimation because she never gave up and still doesn't. She's working hard to keep her man happy and even if to outsiders she appears frivolous and freeloading, I'm guessing, like Bill, she's just playing a part.

Her advice to me is timely because I am already besotted with her son and would probably do anything to keep the flame we ignited alight. But at what cost? She's right to warn me to slow down, although she thinks we've already started running. It's given me a lot to think about and applied the brakes on something that could change my life and I'm not sure if it's for the better or worse.

CHAPTER 27

*J*ulia leaves amid a lot of hugging, kissing and general instruction and as we wave her off at the door, Bill turns and exhales sharply. "Well, now we can relax."

"What's your plan?" Blake looks amused and Bill beams. "I thought a night in front of the game with a huge bowl of popcorn and some beers. You up for that?"

Blake looks disappointed. "I'm sorry. I have a business meeting tonight that I can't really reschedule."

My ears prick up because this is new.

"What about you, Eliza? Do you fancy spending the evening with an old man watching a field of hot athletic bodies get sweaty? I'll throw in some gin if you like."

I make to reply, and Blake says quickly, "Actually, I was going to ask Eliza if she fancied being my plus one."

"Really?"

Blake nods. "I had a call from Marcus Hudson asking if we could meet up. He's bringing his wife along and I wondered if you'd like to make up the numbers."

I am more than excited about this but say casually, "Of course, if it helps."

I don't miss the look Bill gives us before covering it and saying lightly, "Oh well, more popcorn for me then. Don't stay out all night though and corrupt my staff."

He winks at me as he heads inside, and Blake laughs softly. "I think he knows."

"What?"

"That I like you." He spins on his heel before I can react to that and as I scamper after him, I say quickly, "What time?"

"Be ready at seven. I think the table's booked for seven thirty. I'll be going over my notes and prepping for tonight. Sorry to rush off."

I watch him go, Julia's words ringing in my ears. Blake's business is the most important thing to him, and I must remember that. I've been invited to make up the numbers, and that's all and I mustn't read anything more into it than that.

I have a few hours to kill, so decide to take the jeep and pick up some groceries while Blake and Bill are otherwise occupied. Now Julia's left, I can relax a little and will enjoy some alone time and maybe revisit that adorable gift shop again.

It feels good driving into town with the radio on and the sun is shining, which makes everything seem perfect. In fact, the more time I spend in Dream Valley, the more I like it and I'm loving how good I'm feeling. The sea air and sunshine are doing wonders for my mental health, unlike the rather stale air of the office in London and the excruciating commute every day. Maybe everyone should live in a place like this, and perhaps this is where my new beginning lies. I could find a job and stay here when the six months are up. I could offer my domestic services to the residents of Dream Valley or work in one of the local businesses as an assistant. Maybe there's a solicitor here who requires a legal assistant and maybe I should progress my own career in that department.

I brush away the thought of Blake in my future because he will be leaving in two weeks' time to return to the rat race. His is a more lucrative one than mine and I doubt our paths will cross in a year from now.

Just thinking of it makes me sad because I do enjoy his company and that kiss changed everything, well, for me, anyway.

Parking opposite Valley Marketplace, I click the alarm and pull my sunglasses over my eyes.

Heading straight for the gift shop, I love the bright window dressing of scarves, handbags, and jewellery, not to mention the impressive, framed pictures and objects for the home.

As I push my way in, Harriet looks up and smiles. "You came back. How lovely."

"I couldn't stay away for long."

I look with interest at another customer who is lounging on the counter, apparently deep in conversation with the beaming Harriet and as she smiles, I think how pretty she is.

"Hi, I'm Dolly."

She looks so welcoming I instantly like her. "I'm Eliza. I just moved here."

"I heard." She rolls her eyes. "It's all around town how a celebrity of daytime fame is here with a girl young enough to be his daughter."

She lowers her voice as the horror builds in my mind. "You should hear the stories they are spreading; it's entertaining if nothing else."

"Like what?"

"Well…"

Harriett shakes her head and fixes her with a frown. "Don't upset my newest customer, Dolly."

She turns to me and says apologetically. "Nobody thinks anything of it. It's only because people have nothing better to do than gossip."

"I hope so because there really isn't anything to tell. I'm just the housekeeper, nothing more, nothing less."

Dolly nods. "Yes, Mrs Jenkins told us. She's your strongest cheerleader around here and tells it how it is."

"Do you know Dorothy?"

Dolly nods. "She works for my boyfriend's family."

"The Hudsons."

"Yes. I'm dating Brad, their youngest. He's a terrible gossip though, and I wouldn't put it past him to have started the rumours."

"That's interesting. I've met Sammy Jo already and am meeting her husband, Marcus, tonight."

"She's so lovely. Marcus, not quite so much."

"Why? What's wrong with him?"

I feel a little anxious now and Dolly laughs out loud. "If you like the strong, brooding, dominant type, then you'll love Marcus Hudson. It's just a good thing he has Sammy Jo to keep him human. Thanks be to God for that."

"She'd know a lot about thanking God for things." Harriet interrupts. "Dolly's father is the local vicar, and if you're into strong, dominant, alpha males, you wouldn't find a better example than him. Like Sammy Jo though, his wife Tina keeps him on the right path. It's worth heading to the local service for the floor show sometimes."

"Don't remind me." Dolly groans and straightens up. "Anyway, I should go. It's good to meet you, Eliza. We should grab a drink sometime. I'll get your number from Sammy Jo. Oh, and Harriett, I can do Saturday if you need to head off to Wales. Brad is covering the shop and doesn't need my help because we have a new assistant."

She throws me a huge smile as she leaves and as the door closes, Harriet fills me in. "Dolly worked here for a while and covers the shop for me occasionally. Brad owns a travel agent in Riverton and is doing really well as it happens. They are such a lovely couple, and I don't think anybody around here comes close to them. Easy going, good-natured and besotted with each other. Loves young dream, how I envy them that."

Shaking her head, she reverts to business. "Anyway, how can I help you?"

"I'm just browsing, but I doubt I'll leave empty-handed; you appear to have re-stocked."

"Yes, my summer collection arrived and now is the perfect time to take advantage of that before it sells out."

"Is it busy in Dream Valley then? It doesn't appear to be."

"Not now, but when the school holidays kick in, Dreamy Sands Beach is packed with visitors and the caravan park is full. There's also a campsite up at Pineland Forest, which is quite popular, and I heard the other day there are plans to develop Rocky Island."

"Rocky Island?"

My ears prick up because I'm sure Blake would be interested in that bit of news, and she looks excited.

"Yes, it's an island on the other side of Rocky Cove. Currently you can only reach it by boat, but word is it was sold when the owner died and what was once just a refuge for wildlife is now being considered for development."

"It's big then."

"Big enough. I think there's talk of setting it up as a guest-house or campsite. I'm not sure what. It has fabulous views out to sea and would make an exceptional getaway. I even heard it was going to be a five-star hotel or spa. I would be very interested in that."

Wondering if this is what Blake's meeting with Marcus is about, I park the information and just look at the new arrivals, finally deciding on a bright pink scarf and a soft leather purse as birthday gifts for my mother. Thinking of my family, I feel a little homesick and wonder if Bill would mind if I did invite them to stay one weekend, or if they could stay somewhere else and just visit. It's only been a short time though, so I'll ask him in a few weeks once I've settled into my role more.

By the time I head back to Rock House after a very pleasant afternoon, I'm looking forward to trying out a beginner's recipe for shortbread that I googled this morning. Maybe it's time to sharpen my domestic skills and start from the bottom and reinvent myself as a chef. That could be a good career choice and I'd certainly enjoy eating the results, if nothing else.

CHAPTER 28

*I*t feels so good to be dressed for dinner. I've forgotten how great it feels to make the effort and dress up for an occasion. It certainly helps that my companion looks like Blake. My mouth watered when I met him in the living room and took in his white shirt, tucked into smart black trousers with a sturdy brown leather belt around his low-slung hips. His suit jacket looks good on him, and I love the casual way he wears it, looking every inch the successful businessman. As his aftershave wafts across the room and fills my senses, I feel a weakening in my knees as he directs his brooding stare my way that sweeps the length of me with appreciation.

I pulled out all the stops and am so glad I packed my trusty emerald green, velvet cocktail dress. I curled my hair that now shines in waves, and I fixed my make-up to match and ditched my trainers for a pair of black wedges that allow me to walk effortlessly. Unlike those demon stilettos, I could never get the hang of.

Bill whistles when he sees me and says loudly, "Look at you, Eliza, you've transformed like Eliza Doolittle in My Fair Lady. You know, that's one of Julia's favourite movies of all time."

"Mine too." I smile across the room at him, and he grins. "So, back to The Olive Tree. Give my regards to Maria and if you mention my name, she may offer you my discount."

"Your discount?" He laughs at my surprise.

"Julia negotiated it when we visited the other day. She told her that for a discount of ten percent, she would give her a mention on her blog."

"Julia has a blog. How did I not know this?"

Bill nods. "Yes, she embraces technology, unlike me, and has quite a few followers already. She offers tips on recipes, shopping discounts and even has a travel section. You should take a look. I'm quite proud of it. She's an inspiration."

Blake interrupts, "We should be going. I don't want to be late. That's never a good sign when you're wanting to do business."

Bill nods. "Have fun and look after my girl, Blake."

He drops me a wink, which makes me giggle, and as we leave him to his night of pleasure, Blake whispers, "You look amazing, Eliza. I can't stop looking at you."

His words cause a rush of pleasure to pass through me, and I love how he makes me feel. For once, a real man has stepped up; not those side swipes I'm used to who head off on their dates with a hidden agenda.

Blake holds open the passenger door and as I step inside, I feel like Cinderella on her way to the ball. I know she didn't travel there with Prince Charming, but as he drops into the seat beside me it certainly feels that way. I am excited for tonight and for all the possibilities ahead of me and for the first time since I arrived in Dream Valley, I feel the spirit of adventure calling my name to step up and enjoy what happens next.

"I'm looking forward to the meal. I came here with your father, and it was seriously good."

"I'm not surprised he took you there." Blake's low chuckle makes me smile. "He loves Italian food more than anything and mum always limits him to pasta once a week."

"She has his best interests at heart, though." I'm now Julia Monroe's number one fan after our little chat, and Blake nods. "Of course. She idolises my father, and he's much the same about her. It's scarred me a little, if I'm honest."

"Scarred you, why?" I'm amazed and he says slightly wistfully, "It's a lot to live up to and makes me wonder if I'll ever be that lucky. Find my soulmate like they obviously did. You know, I have never seen them argue. Don't you think that's strange?"

"A little."

"I mean, don't get me wrong, mum is always nagging him, but it's done with a good heart and reason. She cares so much for him and sometimes he forgets why she's doing it. He's his own worst enemy and strays a little sometimes."

"Strays! You don't mean..." My eyes are wide, and I'm devastated at the thought and Blake laughs out loud. "Not with women. He never looks at anyone else, flirts maybe, turns on the charm, but never has the same look he reserves only for my mother. I meant food, drink, and exercise. Take tonight, for instance. She would hit the roof if she saw his hand inside a bowl of salty popcorn and his other wrapped around a beer bottle. Don't get me wrong, she knows what he's like, which is why she was happy about our arrangement. She'll be reassured he's eating well and is cared for, and for the next two weeks she'll have someone to report back to her. Don't be surprised if she comes to stay when I leave. I suppose we'll be playing tag with London for a while."

"I can see why." My heart sinks when he mentions leaving and then, to my surprise, he reaches out and takes my hand in his, saying in a voice that feels as if it's caressing my skin, "I don't want to leave; not now."

"You don't?"

"No. I want to stay and see where this leads with us."

"Us?" I'm repeating his words because my mind can't form my own right now and he says slightly huskily, "When I first saw you in that coffee shop, I was blown away. Something clicked inside my brain, and it felt as if I was looking at someone I needed to know."

I am speechless as he presses on. "Hearing you talk made me smile. Finding out more about you became an obsession and from that moment on there were no more applicants for the position. It was as if fate was screaming at me not to let this one pass by and so I'm afraid I engineered everything. I plucked you out of London and placed you where I could keep you to myself. I selfishly decided that the next six months of your life were going to be controlled by me and by the end of it, I would know."

"Know what?"

"Whether we were meant for each other."

I am so shocked I just stare at him, and he raises my hand to his lips and kisses it like a gentleman.

"We're here." He winks and releases me, skilfully manoeuvring the car into a space and as he cuts the engine, he leans across and cups my face in his hands and kisses me with a long, leisurely, soul shattering kiss that leaves me in no doubt at all. I'm in deep already and I had better learn how to swim and fast because something is telling me Blake Monroe is going to change my life and I had better prepare myself for that.

CHAPTER 29

*W*e head inside and outwardly I look calm and collected, but inside I am all over the place. That was so intense. Blake has declared war on my heart, and I am already surrendering. Walking in with him is a delicious experience of happily ever after because it feels as if we were always meant to walk through life together. Don't ask me how I know, I just do, and it feels so natural when he places his hand on the small of my back as we follow Maria to the table where the Hudson's are already waiting.

Sammy Jo jumps up when we approach and hugs me hard, and I love how friendly she always is. There are no reservations with her. She has a genuine warmth that is infectious, and I love how her eyes brim with appreciation when she sees Blake watching the scene with amusement and she whispers, "I'm impressed."

Feeling quite smug, I look past her and almost do a double take because Marcus Hudson is seriously gorgeous, too. Dolly wasn't joking when she referred to him as the brooding type. Dark, dangerous, and reserved with a curious stare and all his emotions locked away. He stands and offers me his hand and then Blake. His grip is firm, and he drawls, "It's good to meet you both. Sammy has told me so much about you. I feel as if I've known you for years."

Sammy Jo giggles and shakes her head. "He's exaggerating. I don't gossip at all."

He laughs out loud and grins at his wife and I love how they stare at one another as if nobody else is looking. Much like Bill and Julia, they appear to have it all worked out, and it gives me hope for my own future, hopefully with Blake.

We take our seats and begin the difficult task of selecting just one starter and main from a menu that offers so much choice. I don't think I will ever run out of options here and I have one ear on the conversation as I struggle to choose.

Maria stops by and she smiles warmly and takes our drinks order and I'm happy to go along with their choice of wine and vow not to drink more than two glasses in case I collapse face first on the table again.

The fact Blake leans closer and discusses my choices in a low voice makes me feel warm inside. It's as if we are a couple, like Sammy Jo and Marcus, who are doing much the same. His arm casually wrapped around her shoulders as they huddle over her menu, and she points various things out.

The candle flickers on the table and the lighting is dim. It feels quite romantic and as moments go, I don't want this one to end. Could this be my future? Dining out with friends on a similar journey to mine. Will Blake and I make it through and begin something that could lead to an exciting future? Right now, in this moment, it certainly does feel like the beginning of something. The starting point for potentially a happy future and with a man like Blake beside me, I have every reason to be happy about that.

Once our selections are made, Marcus turns the conversation to business, which is, after all, the reason we are here. I listen in awe as they discuss their plans for Dream Valley Heights and am surprised that Sammy Jo is every bit as involved as her husband. They are obviously a great team because one bounces off the other and I love that they work so well together. Sammy Jo came to Dream Valley as Marcus's assistant, among other things, and she dropped many interesting details about what happened next that astonished me. Somehow, they ended up marrying and are living out their happily ever after in style, which gives me hope.

By the sounds of things, Marcus is keen for Blake to invest in his project in return for first choice on three rental properties, with the option for more in future developments. In return, Blake will set up an investment portfolio and between them they will invest the money in hedge funds that will hopefully see rapid growth, rather than leaving the money in the bank where there is almost zero to be made. It all sounds complicated to me and it's only when they start discussing future developments, I chip in.

"Do you have anything to do with the development of Rocky Island?"

Marcus looks surprised. "How do you know about that?"

"I heard about it in that lovely gift shop. The owner told me about it."

"Harriet." Sammy looks at her husband. "Did you know about this?"

He looks thoughtful. "I did hear some mention of it when I met Elspeth Grainger of the planning committee."

Sammy Jo shivers. "That woman scares the hell out of me."

Marcus laughs. "She's ok when you get used to her ways."

Sammy says with interest, "So what's happening with Rocky Island? I thought it was in private hands."

"Apparently the owner died, and his successor is keen to sell it, but there's a codicil in the will forbidding it for ten years, so they decided to capitalise on their asset and do something with it."

"Do they need investors?"

Blake's ears prick up and I regret not mentioning it before.

"I'm not sure. To be honest, it's only just happened, and I'm surprised that word is out already. I don't even know who the owner is."

"I'll do some digging." Blake takes a sip of his wine, and I can tell he's excited about that. It's obvious he loves his job and thrives on it.

All talk of business is soon forgotten when the food arrives and as we tuck in, I can't think of anything else but how lovely it tastes. Blake feeds me samples of his own dishes for my approval, and I do the same to him. I don't miss Sammy's amused expression as she watches us and yet she can talk because she is doing much the same. It feels as if we're on a double date, which I am more than happy about.

While we wait for the second course, Marcus says to me, "What are your plans, Eliza? Sammy tells me you're here for six months. What happens after that?"

Blake reaches under the table and squeezes my hand, and I wonder if he is thinking the same thing.

"I don't know. I came here looking for a fresh start, knowing it would be temporary. I'm open to offers though and am lucky, I guess, because I could do anything."

Sammy looks at Blake and says slyly, "What about you Blake, are you looking for a new beginning too?"

I hold my breath as I wait for his answer and he squeezes my hand and says in a firm voice, "Like Eliza, I'm at a turning point. I'm happy in my job. I love what I do, and I would be a fool to walk away from my position in the city. But I'm discovering there's more to life than working and I'm keen to develop more balance in my life. Maybe a place like Dream Valley is the perfect place to escape from it all and I am seriously considering purchasing my own bolthole away from London and this could be the perfect place for that."

"You are?" This is the first I've heard of this, and he nods, his eyes sparkling with something I can't quite place. "Yes, being away from London has taught me there's a lot of value in distance. I can work from home, and it's made me look at things differently. Some of the guys at work split their time between home and the office, and I may do the same. It gives me more time to concentrate without the distractions of the office and frees up more time to relax."

Sammy Jo looks happy. "That's great news. I do hope you choose Dream Valley; we would love you to move here even if it is for a few days a month. This is what Marcus wanted when he decided to develop his family's land. To increase the population and ensure the prosperity of Dream Valley in a way that doesn't detract from its beauty."

She smiles and I don't miss the glint in her eye as she says mischievously, "Maybe Eliza can find a job here, too. I'm sure we could come up with something between us."

Marcus looks thoughtful. "Leave it with me. Sammy tells me you're a legal secretary when you're not taking a break. Is that something you wish to continue?"

"Possibly, although I did wonder if I should train to be a solicitor."

"You did?" Blake looks surprised and I shrug. "It was a conversation I had with your mother. She advised me to look at my own future and plan it. I thought about what she said and she's right. I need to make the most of my skills and as much as I love keeping house, I'm not that good at it — yet anyway. I do love the legal side of things, so was thinking I may study and take a job to pay my way as I qualify to take a step up."

Marcus says quickly, "There's a solicitor I use in Riverton. I could always put in a good word for you. The owner is a good friend of mine."

Sammy nods enthusiastically. "Yes, that would be amazing, Eliza. We would help you find a place to stay. We manage so many rentals it would be easy."

Blake's hold on my hand is almost crushing it, and I wonder if he's happy where this conversation is going. He's so difficult to read and as the main course arrives and everyone is momentarily distracted, he whispers, "We need to talk."

A small flutter inside is growing as I see the passion in his eyes, and I wonder what he wants to talk about. One thing's for sure, something is building fast between us, and I am both fearful and excited about what that may involve.

The rest of the evening is fun because now the business has been discussed we talk about more personal issues. Sammy Jo tells us all about the people who live here and when she mentions Jim, the taxi driver, it makes me giggle as I recite my own experience in his cab. She tells me how Dolly and her family caused quite a stir when they first arrived and all about Marcus's brother Jake and his fiancée Florence, who was the reason Sammy Jo met Marcus at all. Apparently, they all met on a cruise, and both Florence and Sammy Jo relocated to Dream Valley to live at Valley House.

It certainly seems that Dream Valley is a special place where dreams come true and new beginnings are made and I'm hopeful that some of its magic rubs off on me and Blake because the more time I spend with him, the deeper I am falling.

CHAPTER 30

*A*fter an extremely pleasant evening, we head off and I'm feeling quite tipsy. Blake stuck to one glass of wine and water and I'm glad of his strong arm of support as we bid Sammy Jo and Marcus farewell and head towards the jeep.

The fresh air is welcome after the warm and cosy restaurant and as we reach the car, I lean back against the door with a sigh of relief.

"I think I've had too much wine."

I can feel the heat spreading through my body as the alcohol wraps me in a contented glow and Blake says in his husky voice, "That's a shame."

"What is?"

"That you're over the limit. I was hoping to corrupt you a little more, and now it would feel as if I was taking advantage of you."

"Corrupt me, how?" My ears prick up because I'm up for a bit of corruption, as long as it's him providing it, and he laughs. "I hoped we could try out the hot tub. It's such a beautiful night, I thought it would be great to sip champagne in the tub, under the stars, while listening to the ocean."

"Sold." I grin and immediately try to sober up. "I'm up for that."

He opens the door and helps me into my seat and whispers, "Then so am I."

As he starts the engine, I feel a shiver of excitement pass through me. A hot tub, with Blake and champagne. Can this night get any better?

My heart is thumping with anticipation as we make the brief journey back to Rock House and I steal brief glances at the man who is running away with my heart, and I am struggling to keep up. It's a powerful feeling – attraction. It makes rational thought almost impossible, and I know my heart is lost already, which should worry me because I'm liable to make a fool of myself. However, this is my new beginning. A brand-new age where Eliza Benson lives her best life and if nothing happens past a frolic in a hot tub with the man of my dreams, at least I'll have a delicious memory to treasure of the time I let my guard down and lived.

* * *

The house is in darkness when we return, telling me that Bill has retired already and as we head inside, Blake says, "I'll leave you to change and meet you on the deck outside."

"OK."

I feel a little shy now in the house's silence and know that something magical is about to happen because I can see it in his eyes. They burn with emotion and desire and it's a powerful weapon because I couldn't back out now if I tried.

Luckily, I brought a few bikinis and swimsuits with me, anticipating a dip in the sea during my stay and so I wrap my dressing gown around me and head outside, a slight fluttering of nerves playing on my emotions. I'm not sure what I want to happen tonight, but I'm hoping for something romantic, at least. It surprises me how quickly I've developed feelings for Blake when he irritated me almost on sight just a few days ago. Things are moving fast, and I should apply the brakes, but what if he leaves in just over a week's time and things fizzle out? Distance has a habit of doing that and so I must keep my guard in place because I'm guessing one taste of forbidden fruit is all it would take to change things in a heartbeat.

My eyes widen when I step outside and see candles lit in lanterns set all around, their flames dancing as they are protected from the cool breeze. The waves are crashing into shore, adding drama to the occasion, and my heart races when I see Blake standing in a bathrobe that's open to the waist, uncorking a bottle of champagne that he has plucked from an ice bucket on a stand.

Our eyes meet across the dimly lit space and the way he lazily drags his eyes the length of me with a heated expression makes my knees weak and my resolve shattered beneath my feet. His intentions are obvious because this is seduction at its finest. Is this something he does all the time? A practised routine to spend a pleasant evening. Will he throw the memory on the pile when he heads back to business and his one true love — making money?

I couldn't care less actually because I'm going to enjoy every minute of this and as he offers me a glass of champagne, I head across to accept it gratefully.

"This is—"

"Romantic?" He laughs softly. "I just thought I'd create atmosphere."

"It worked."

As I sip the cool champagne, I wonder how my life ended up like this. Sipping the posh stuff with a man so far out of my league, it's not even funny. If only my mum could see me now, she would be ecstatic.

"This is nice." I wave my hand around and smile, loving every second of what's happening.

"It is. I thought I should pull out all the stops to impress you."

"You want to impress me? I like the sound of that."

"Why wouldn't I?"

"Of course, why wouldn't you? I am amazing, after all."

I grin to take the conceit from my words and his eyes sparkle in the moonlight as he says huskily, "Shall we?"

He points to the hot tub and then slowly removes his robe and I shamelessly ogle a body I need to feel in my arms immediately.

Swallowing hard, I do the same and make a mad dash for the tub, breaking our connection and submerging my body under the hot, bubbling water.

He seems almost amused as he joins me and settles beside me with one arm resting casually behind and one hand holding the champagne flute with casual ease.

Me, I cling onto my glass as if it's my lifeline and don't just sip the bubbles, I gulp them down, which causes me to cough uncontrollably.

It takes a minute to get my breath and Blake's low laugh beside me makes me grin. "Sorry about that. It went down too fast."

To my surprise, he reaches down and takes my glass from my hands and sets it alongside his on the edge and then turning, runs his hand behind my head and pulls my face to his in a powerful gesture of dominance that takes my breath away. He doesn't even speak and just steals a kiss as if it's his by rights and as we cement whatever this is, I couldn't care less about anything other than him right now.

Kissing Blake in a hot tub with the taste of champagne fresh on my lips is the best thing I have ever done in my life. It's magical, even, and I am reluctant for this night to end. So many emotions are controlling me without my permission because my inner cheerleader replaces every warning I have ever heard, telling me to seize the moment *and* the man.

We kiss, we touch, and we enjoy a leisurely night under the stars. In between kisses, we talk in low voices about the future, our hopes, dreams and past, and I'm surprised when the light changes and dawn is already on the horizon.

"What time is it?" I lift my head from Blake's shoulder. We progressed from the hot tub a few hours ago and wrapped ourselves in our robes and blankets and fell asleep on the double day bed.

"Sunrise."

Blake shifts to a sitting position and pulls me up, wrapping his arms around me in a Bear hug as we watch the sun make its journey to replace the moon.

"We should make a wish." I've always been impetuous, and he says with amusement, "I know what mine is."

"Then close your eyes and wish hard but keep it to yourself, otherwise it won't come true."

I do the same and sneakily open one eye to check he's following instruction and laugh to myself when I see his eyes tightly closed and the concentration on his face.

Quickly shutting my own eyes, I think about what I want most in the world and push aside world peace and health just for more moments like this with Blake. A lifetime of them actually because I've always asked for more than I should, just ask Santa and as the sun rises, so do my hopes of a happily ever after with the man beside me.

"This has been nice." Blake's voice brings an end to our night of pleasure, and I sigh. "It was amazing."

"You're amazing." He drops a light kiss on the top of my head and pulls me close, wrapping me in his muscular arms just like I dreamed of a few hours ago.

"I should shower and change. Bill will be up soon and want food."

"I'll help if you like."

"Really."

"You sound surprised."

"I am a little. It's nice though."

"Good, because despite your first impressions, I'm not completely useless and to confirm my first ones of you, you are."

He laughs as I shove him hard, and yet I can't wipe the huge grin from my face as I enjoy every minute of this.

"Come on then, I have work to do."

Sighing, he pulls me up from the daybed and as we walk hand in hand into the house, I wish I could bottle up this moment and keep it forever, marked the happiest night of my life.

CHAPTER 31

*O*ver the next few days, life settles into a pattern of domestic bliss. Blake helps me with breakfast and then, while I clear away, he starts work either in the living room or out on the veranda. Bill is good company, and we enjoy cohabiting in a relaxed and informal way. The house is full of laughter, and it feels like nothing could ever burst the bubble we have created.

Blake and I enjoy endless walks along the beach and many nice visits to town, where we love tucking ourselves in the Cosy Kettle and trying out all the cakes on offer. Harriet is doing well from my addiction to her shop and I'm certain Valley Market-place's profits have gone up since Bill came to town because he is always dropping by for more forbidden snacks and alcohol, making Alice Bevan's day at the same time.

Sammy Jo and Marcus are becoming good friends and as the deadline for Blake's stay here looms, a feeling of dread is rising within me. I'm not sure why, but this all feels too good to be true and, as it turns out, it is.

My phone rings while I'm folding laundry because out of everything, this is the only thing I excel at.

"Hi, mum. How are things?"

"Good thanks. I thought I'd give you a quick call while your father is down at the surgery having his blow job."

I'm sorry. There's that moment when you question your own sanity, and this is definitely one of those, and mum says with a flicker of impatience. *"You know, for his asthma. They get him to blow into one of those puffy things and measure his readings."*

My heart sags with relief because I know you can get most things on the NHS these days, but blow jobs are a step too far in my opinion.

"Anyway, Margaret Mountjoy was talking the other day and asked after you. Apparently, she ran into a colleague of yours in Poundland and they mentioned your old job was still going. She asked me to mention it to you because her friend is run off her feet with work and Mr Henderson is so fussy none of the temps are cutting it and leave after the first day."

"Oh, I didn't know Margaret knew Miss Travers?"

Thinking of my former colleague, I wonder again how she's stuck working there so long and mum sighs.

"Yes, they go to ballroom dancing together. There's a shortage of men in their class and Margaret likes to play the man and lead."

"Sounds, um, interesting. Maybe you and dad…"

"Never in a month of Sundays." Mum says quickly.

"Anyway, I just thought I'd pass on the good news that your old job is still going. Apparently, Mr Henderson can't stop talking about you and how amazing you were, which makes all the others feel inferior and unable to measure up. It made me so proud, love, I can't tell you and I even had a teary moment when I thought of how well you've done. It got me thinking that you shouldn't throw away your gift and become a domestic slave for the rich and famous."

"I thought you were happy about that. It is for your idol, after all."

"I suppose. Has he asked after me yet? Maybe asked you to engineer a meeting so he can check me out?"

"No mum, he hasn't."

"Perhaps I should pay you that visit you keep on asking me for."

"I don't." I roll my eyes despite the fact she can't see me, and mum says, sounding a little disappointed, *"Well, don't make it too long. I could really do with a break; your father is in one of his moods again."*

"Why?"

"He's bored with doing your room and says it's ruining his life. Why are men always so dramatic? Just because he's been tinkering with it for nearly two weeks now, that doesn't constitute ruining anyone's life. In fact, if he wasn't so pedantic over every brush stroke, he would have had it done in a couple of days and be onto the next thing by now. Trust my luck to be married to a perfectionist, or a procrastinator more likely."

"Does it look nice?" I'm quite excited to see my new room and wonder if it will be like one of those big reveals you see on the television. I'm imagining loft style chic and possibly one of those feature walls with a huge custom-made design, flowers probably with a swirl of glitter in the detail. I feel quite excited about that, and mum says with an air of boredom, *"We went with magnolia. You can't beat a blank canvas."*

Luckily, I'm saved from this conversation by the doorbell ringing and wonder if Blake and Bill forgot their key. They went to Pineland Forest for a hike after breakfast, and even though I was invited, I was more than happy to say I had too much work to do. I've never been one for extreme sports and they looked as if they were conquering Mount Everest judging by their walking boots, backpacks, and thermos flask. I was more than happy to enjoy some peace and quiet, and then my mother had to interrupt with her ramblings.

"Sorry mum, I've got to go. There's someone at the door."

"Don't open it."

"Why not?" I laugh to myself as mum says in a whisper, *"Peer out of the window first and check it's not a murderer. You hear all sorts about young vulnerable women on their own and it's a stalker's paradise waiting to happen."*

"Mum, I don't have a stalker and if I did, I doubt he would have found me in Dream Valley. I don't think this place is even on the map."

Laughing to myself, I say a cheery, "Love you, speak soon." and cut the call, giggling to myself as I make my way to answer the door that is ringing again, telling me the person outside is an impatient one.

Ignoring my mother's advice, I fling open the door and am surprised to see an attractive woman waiting. She has long dark hair and flashing green eyes and is wearing a smart pink suit that looks amazing on her.

"Oh, hi, may I help you?" I smile but feel uncomfortable at the way she drags her gaze the length of me and sneers, "Is Blake in?"

My heart lurches as I sense something coming that I'm not going to like.

"I'm afraid not. Shall I tell him who was asking?"

"I'll wait." She pushes past me before I can object and I follow her into the room, stuttering, "I'm sorry, but you can't just push your way in here. I'll tell him you called, but I must ask you to leave."

She turns and throws me a supercilious look and snarls, "How dare you question me? You're just a common servant."

"Please leave." I am now furious and will not be spoken to like this and she laughs dismissively and says coldly, "It is I who must ask you to leave."

"But…"

I'm so taken aback I can't form a reply, and she laughs, sounding a little crazy. "Listen, I don't take kindly to your attitude and if you knew who I was, you would be a little more polite."

"Is that so? Then please enlighten me."

I am now sincerely regretting not listening to my mother's advice and then she destroys my bubble with a perfectly aimed dart of destruction.

"I'm Blake's wife, Erin, and what I want to know is, who the hell are you?"

CHAPTER 32

*M*y world has stopped spinning and self-destructed. I can only stare at the fuming woman before me and battle the tears in my eyes.

He's married and never thought I should know. Why didn't his parents warn me? I can excuse Bill because he doesn't know we are dating. Well, not at first, but he certainly does now. But Julia, surely, she would have told me. Something doesn't add up.

"I asked you a question." Her sharp voice sticks the knife further in and I mumble, "Eliza. The housekeeper."

"Then fetch me some tea while I wait for my husband and make sure it's green tea. I can't stomach the working-class kind that you probably enjoy."

Blinking back the tears, I shake my head and try to inject some authority into my voice.

"I'm sorry. My request still stands. I must ask you to leave."

"Are you stupid or something?" She gazes at me as if I have two heads and I rustle up every ounce of my dignity and say roughly, "No. I'm a human being who deserves some respect. You don't appear to have that capability, so I must ask you to wait outside."

"How dare you?" She faces me with all the fury of a woman used to getting what she wants and I'm almost watching this scene unfold like an interested observer because I feel strangely detached from the whole situation.

Wondering if I'll have to physically fight this woman, I'm saved by the return of Blake and Bill, who head inside the door with a cheery, "Eliza, we're home."

If anything, I see a little fear enter Erin's eyes and then as Blake heads into the room, I watch his face fall and his eyes blink in surprise as he says in disbelief, "Oh my god, Erin. What are you doing here?"

Taking that as my cue to leave, I don't even look at him and say tightly, "If you'll excuse me."

The fact he calls my name doesn't stop me and I head through the bifold doors and race down the steps to the beach below. Blake's voice follows me as he calls for me to come back, but I don't care. I need to remove myself from this situation as quickly as possible. Blake has a wife, and she's come to stay, and they never even told me. I feel like such a fool and as the tears blind my vision, I run along the beach, not sure of where I'm going except as far away from Rock House as possible.

I'm not even sure how far I walk, or how long it's been because all I can think of is her. Why didn't he tell me? Even if they are apart, he surely would have told me. The fact she's here tells me they have unfinished business. Perhaps they are still together, but my heart tells me they can't be. He still lives at home and even his parents haven't mentioned her. Maybe she's a secret wife that he has yet to mention. Perhaps they married in haste and she's pregnant with his child. So many scenarios battle in my mind and I believe every single one of them, no matter how implausible they seem.

I soon grow tired and flop down onto the sand and draw my knees to my chest. The tears are falling, but I don't check them. I just stare blindly out at sea because if anything, I feel used. I'm just the hired help that's good for a bit of fooling around. Thank goodness we never took it further than a few kisses and cuddles. I really thought he was different from the rest. Honest, dependable, and one of the good ones. However, it turns out he's hiding secrets in imaginary little boxes marked 'confidential' because who doesn't mention a wife, either current or past, when carrying on with another woman?

I'm not sure what to do now because I've left in a moment of panic and don't want to go back while she's there, so I do the only thing I can and start walking in the direction of Dream Valley town. It's only fifteen minutes by road, but I'm hoping there's a shortcut along the coastal path and there's only one place I feel I can go. Harriett's shop where I can ask her to call Sammy Jo. Maybe she will offer me some words of advice. I could certainly use some right now.

My turbulent thoughts are my only companion as I power walk through my misery. I know I'm a coward for not sticking around, but I couldn't bear to face the truth. What if they are happy and Blake's cheating on his wife? It could be possible, and she found out and came in all guns blazing. I know I would.

I feel so miserable and worthless, good for nothing and a fool. Maybe I should head back to London and my old job. As it turns out, new beginnings aren't that great, anyway.

I finally reach town and feel my weary limbs screaming in protest. It's taken me two hours to reach a place that seems as if it's only up the road from Rock House.

Just my luck. The first person I see is Gerry, hauling shopping into a pickup truck that's double parked.

"Hey, Eliza." My heart sinks as he heads my way and when he reaches me, I'm surprised at the concern in his eyes. "Are you ok? I think they're looking for you."

"Who are?"

"That famous actor and his son. They told us we're to call them if you show up."

"You won't, will you?"

I feel worried and it must show because he shrugs, "Not if you don't want me to."

His kindness brings the tears to my eyes, and he says with concern, "Are you ok?"

"Not really, Gerry."

"Can I help?" This causes fresh tears to appear because why have I been so dismissive of him just because Mrs Bevan told me he was sweet on me? I feel like such a bitch and say through my tears, "I don't suppose you could give me a lift to Sammy Jo's house. Do you think she'd be there, or maybe where she works?"

"Sure, I was just going on my deliveries. I'll take you to find her."

"Thanks, Gerry, I'm really grateful."

"It's fine. I'd do anything for you, Eliza."

The look he gives me makes my heart openly weep because why is he so lovely and why can't I fall in love with a man like him? Genuine, caring, and hardworking, just lacking the part where I'm attracted to him.

He guides me to the passenger side of his truck, and I don't really care about my safety at getting into a stranger's car because it's Gerry. I know him, although my judgement is in question after what happened today.

Gerry's truck needs a good valet and the rather pungent odour of meat filled pastries almost overwhelms me as we head out of town. I see the remnants of his lunch in a crushed paper bag on the dashboard and shudder when I see a few crumbs littering the seats and centre console. In fact, there are many discarded take out cups and various crisp wrappers tucked in the side of the door and decorating the floor. I wish he would open the window because it's making me feel nauseous and yet his cheery voice cuts through my misery as he says, "If you want my advice, I'd look for another job."

"You would?" It almost makes me smile as he says cheerily, "I could put in a good word with my aunt if you like. We could use help at the store on the weekend."

"Thanks, I'll bear it in mind." It cheers me up because every dark cloud has a new horizon and working in Valley Marketplace may not be my life's ambition, but it's a start at least.

"I never trust those city types. Shifty, if you ask me."

"Does that include me?" I laugh softly and he shakes his head vigorously. "Not you, Eliza, you're perfect."

The mist falls across my eyes once again and I say with a hitch to my voice, "What about you, Gerry? Are you married? Do you have a girlfriend and how long have you worked at the store?"

"No, no, and five years." He grins, revealing a crooked smile that's quite infectious.

"I dated Desiree Blunden for a year. It was going well until she got a job in a care home in Eastbourne ."

"That must have been hard."

"For her, not me."

"Why not?"

"Because I got to stay in Dream Valley. It's the best place to live, in my opinion."

"Then you must be pleased they're developing it. There will be lots more customers for your shop.'

"I suppose, but not everyone is happy."

"I understand that nobody likes change."

He nods and then fixes me with a look of yearning. "Maybe you can buy one, Eliza. I could show you around."

"I don't think I can afford one on a housekeeper's salary."

Gerry nods. "I know what you mean. It's hard to earn enough money to buy nice things. I live above the shop with my aunt, and I can't see a way out of that."

It appears that Gerry and I are no different, really. Neither of us has a grand plan and are just letting life carry them along. At least I have the potential to make a career, I suppose, and I wonder if Gerry has ambitions of his own.

"What about you? What did you always want to be?"

"A fireman." He says it with pride, which makes me smile.

"Then you should go for it."

"I have asthma. They won't let me apply because of it."

"I'm so sorry."

He shrugs. "It's fine. I'm thinking of starting my own business, anyway."

"Doing what?" This is interesting, and I smile with encouragement.

"Gardening. If Marcus Hudson gets his wish and several new homes spring up, they may want someone to look after their garden."

"You should definitely do that; it sounds a good plan."

We sit in silence for a bit and then Gerry surprises me by saying with a gentle edge to his voice, "I think that guy really likes you, Eliza."

"Who?" I pretend not to know, and he says slightly enviously, "That actor's son. I could see he was anxious when he came into the shop."

"He was?"

"Yes. He looked upset. It must be nice to have someone who likes you that much."

"I suppose."

Thinking about Blake brings a fresh burst of disappointment. I was falling in love with him. So quickly and completely and I feel betrayed by my own judgement. Most of all, though, I feel like a fool for running. I didn't even wait to see what happened and if I feel anything it's regret about that and so I make a decision that I suppose was always necessary.

"Gerry," my voice has a steely ring locked around it and I say with a deep breath, "Change of plan. Could you drop me off at Rock House?"

"Are you sure?" He looks concerned and I smile bravely. "My mother always taught me to never run away from things and face them head on. I forgot that for a moment, and now I need to deal with this in the right way."

"Does it have anything to do with that strange woman?"

"Woman?" My heart starts racing as he sneers. "Typical posh bird from the city. She walked into our store like she owned it and pushed in front of Mrs Kryton and demanded to know where Bill Monroe was staying."

"She asked for Bill?" I'm surprised, and he shakes his head. "My aunt told her she didn't know anything about a Bill Monroe and if she wasn't buying anything to get out of her shop."

"I wonder why she asked?" I'm surprised at that because I would have thought she knew already.

Once again, something isn't adding up and the need for answers is even stronger now.

"How long before we get there?"

"Ten minutes."

"I'm not taking you out of your way, am I?" I feel bad for messing him around and he says with a sad tone to his voice, "I'd do anything for you, Eliza. I told you."

"You're a good friend, Gerry."

I really mean that and vow to be a kinder person in the future. Why did I make a rash judgement on him just because of what his aunt said and why was that such a bad thing, anyway? I avoided him and shied away from conversation when I did see him and all because I thought I deserved better and had a high opinion of myself. I feel ashamed and am fast realising that the people of Dream Valley don't have hidden agendas. They are open, honest, and welcoming and are way better people than I'll ever be. Maybe I should learn this lesson and keep it close because if anything has changed my attitude on life, it's the amazing locals who live here.

CHAPTER 33

They must hear Gerry's truck because as soon as we come to a stop, Blake rushes out. I notice the jeep is missing and say quickly, "Where's Bill?" More importantly, I notice that Erin's car has gone, which makes me sigh with relief.

Blake races across and grips me hard, as if he's never letting go. "Thank God you came back."

Gerry is watching the scene with curiosity, and I pull away from Blake and smile at him apologetically. "Thank you so much, Gerry. I really appreciate the ride and the chat. Maybe I can buy you a drink to say thanks."

His face brightens, and he nods vigorously. "Great, I'd like that, Eliza."

"I'll come and find you."

He smiles such a beautiful smile it makes me feel better about myself and as he heads off, Blake says in a puzzled voice. "What have I missed?"

The confusion in his eyes is nothing to what's happening inside me right now, and I say with a sigh. "Maybe we should talk."

"Of course, yes, you probably have questions."

"You could say that. Firstly, where's Bill?"

"Looking for you. He's driving around Dream Valley in the hope of finding you. We were so worried."

"Why?"

"Because of Erin, I suppose. I didn't want you to get the wrong idea, and when you ran off, I was torn between chasing you and getting rid of her."

"Getting rid of her, but she's your wife."

Blake groans and says in a tortured voice, "She said that. No wonder you ran off. Come on, I need a stiff drink and I think you will too."

We head straight to the kitchen and as he pours two large shots into the glasses and adds tonic, I wonder if this is the cure for everything in the Monroe household.

Grabbing the drinks, he says with a sigh, "Let's take this outside. You're probably not going to believe this but keep an open mind and trust that I'm telling you the truth."

I watch as he sets the glasses down on the table and removes his phone with a quick, "I'll text dad and call off the search."

I feel bad that Bill is driving around town in his condition and hope I'm not the cause of more health issues. I really do feel like a fool for racing off like that and know I've learned a thousand important lessons today about growing up and acting like an adult.

Blake pulls me beside him on the daybed and sighs heavily. "What a day."

"Are you going to tell me about it?"

"It's quite a disturbing story, but one I should have told you, more to warn you, I suppose."

Something is telling me I'm not going to like what I hear next, and Blake takes a swig of his drink and sighs. "Erin was someone I dated. One night was enough to tell me she seriously strange."

"But you married her." I am so confused, and he shakes his head with an emphatic. "No, I did not."

"But she said she was your wife."

"It doesn't mean she is. You see, Erin, as it turns out, is a woman with issues, for want of a better word. We met at a pub on the embankment and after a few drinks, I got seriously weird vibes from her. She was staring at me as if I was all her dreams come true and was more forward than I was comfortable with."

"In what way?"

"Well, she kept placing her foot on vulnerable areas under the table and asking me if it felt good."

My mouth twitches as he says in a tortured voice, "She was over the top suggestive and asked me if I wanted to spend the night at her flat. I politely declined, but she either didn't hear me or didn't want to. I made my excuses to leave because she kept on taking photos of me on her phone and even leaned over the table and snapped us together. Then she started talking about what our wedding would be like and how many children we would have. To be blunt, she was making no secret of her plans and I was on edge the whole time."

He leans back and takes a gulp of courage and says, "When it got late, I asked if I could call her a cab and she told me she would rather come home with me. Luckily, I played the 'living at home' card, but she just told me she would have to meet her in laws at some point, so it may as well be now."

I can't help it and just start laughing because the look on his face is priceless. Just imagining him trying to get out of the whole situation is so funny. I wish I could have seen it for myself.

Blake groans even louder. "It gets worse."

"Surely not." I can't imagine how and he takes another swig of his drink and exhales sharply. "The next day at work I had a call from reception telling me my wife was downstairs to meet me for lunch."

"No way."

I can't believe it and he looks as if he's seen a ghost. "I told her I didn't have a wife and wasn't expecting anyone and then I was told she said I would say that, and I shouldn't let a domestic disagreement prevent us from making up. The receptionist was feeling uncomfortable. I could tell it in her voice, and I didn't want Erin to make a scene, so I went downstairs."

"What happened?" This is like one of Bill's drama episodes and I am so invested in this story.

"I took her aside and told her to stop kidding around. I tried to let her down gently and said I wasn't looking for anything past the first date. Then she started crying, actually it was more like wailing and began hitting me as if I had broken her heart."

"Wow, what happened? Did they call the police?"

"Of course not. To everyone watching, I was now public enemy number one, so I had to take her out for a coffee just to calm her down. Anyway, I thought it had worked when I told her she wasn't my type and to move on. I wasn't interested. I tried to let her down gently, and I thought I'd got through because she just looked at me sadly and turned and walked away."

"So, what went wrong?"

"I started getting calls at work where she threatened to end her life if I didn't give in to my feelings for her. She turned up when I arrived at work and was there in the coffee shop waiting for me to leave. She became such a nuisance I called the police and took out a restraining order against her, but she even started wearing wigs and disguises, popping up at places I went to and interrupting dates I had. She even attacked one woman I was on a date with when she went to the ladies, and I only knew when the girl threw a glass of wine in my face and told me my wife had just slapped her for having an affair with her husband. I couldn't even explain before she stormed out, calling me every name under the sun. I got a few looks then too and felt like an idiot while I mopped off the wine and paid the bill."

"I'm so sorry, Blake, that's terrible."

"It got worse."

"No way."

"I'm afraid so. She became a regular where I worked and started stalking me online. She created a fake Facebook page where we were a couple. I think she called it Blake and Erin forever."

I try to stop laughing, but I can't, and he sighs heavily. "Somehow, she started sending all my friends' friend requests on Facebook. Some even followed her, thinking we were an item. She had photographs of us doing things like any other couple. Days out, romantic walks and holidays. There were even photos of our lovely home and pictures of baby scans. The whole thing was an elaborate lie, a make-believe world that she used technology to verify. My friends were confused and starting second guessing me. It all seemed so unbelievable when I told them. The evidence was staring them in the face every time they signed into Facebook, and even the restraining order didn't shut her profile down. It was a horrible situation that wasn't going away, and I threw myself into my work to block it out. I deleted my social profiles and became a recluse, preferring the security of my parent's home rather than the rental I had near the office."

He turns to me and says with so much anguish, I feel bad for him. "Please believe me, Eliza, it was one disastrous date from a dating app. I suppose when I overheard your own experience, I felt we shared something in common. The thought of you going through the same thing filled me with terror and so I decided to save you from that. At least that was my intention, but as it turned out, I just dropped you into the madness with me. When I think of what she could have done, I can't tell you how scared I was. I had to find you, but not before I got rid of her once and for all."

"What did you do?" I'm almost afraid to ask, and he says grimly, "I told her that if she didn't leave me alone, I would go public. My father is famous and has the ear of every daytime talk show there is. I would splurge her name across social media and start a campaign on stalkers and people who commit fraud online. I promised I would make an example of her and by the time I had finished, she would be locked up in a mental institution. I also told her I had moved on and was crazy stupid in love with the most fantastic woman in the world and was intending on spending the rest of my life with her."

"You said what?" My mouth drops and his eyes soften, and he whispers, "I fell in love with you, Eliza. If I'm honest, I fell in love with you in that coffee shop across the street from your own personal hell. I fell in love with your attitude to life, your quirky ways, and your eccentric behaviour. I fell in love with how kind you are and how you made a friend of my father. There is nothing I don't love about you, and the thought of you not being in my life scares me even more than Erin."

We grin like idiots, and he brushes his lips against mine and says huskily, "I want to make a life with you and I'm not sure how that will work, but if you want it too, we'll make it happen."

"I do."

I can't believe what I'm hearing and say with a smile, "I do want that, Blake. Surprisingly, I saw past that cocky attitude, arrogant behaviour, and dubious personality. I dismissed the mummy's boy, who still lived at home and only cared about money. I saw the man behind the designer clothes and recognised someone I don't want to live without and most of all, I have discovered I'm nothing like Annalise Turtle because I want only one man in my life forever, and I'm looking at him."

No more words are necessary because somehow, we have arrived on the same page. We both want the same thing and that's each other. We kiss like there's no more time to waste and as the stars align and the planets shift, dreams do come true, and we have the rest of our lives to make more, together.

EPILOGUE

SIX MONTHS LATER

*B*lake holds my hand as we stare out at the skyline, and it feels a million miles away from Dream Valley.

"Are you happy?" He squeezes my hand, and as I hear the concern in his voice, it makes me smile because Blake only appears happy if I am.

"I am. I never thought I'd end up here, back where I started, but it's a temporary visa I suppose."

He drapes his arm around my shoulder and pulls me close, the glint of his crystal glass catching the light from the lamp on the table beside us.

"Are you ok about tomorrow?"

"A little nervous, but I'll be fine."

When our time was up in Rock House, we all packed up and returned to London. I went home to live with my parents, and Blake did the same. That was exactly four weeks ago, which gave us enough time to sort things out and arrange our future.

"Dad's happy to be back at work."

"I can tell." We see the reflection in the window of his parents laughing at something my mum is telling them, and I inwardly groan. "I really hope she's not embarrassing me over there."

"Probably more like the other way around. My father dines out on embarrassing stories about my puberty years. It's probably best we stay here."

He tightens his grip and whispers, "No regrets."

"Of course not."

"We will go back."

"I'm counting on it."

When we said our goodbyes to Dream Valley, it was with the promise of coming back. As soon as the houses are ready, we have one with our name on it. Until then, we are renting Blake's previous flat in London, and he is working hard. I start at a solicitor's office in the Strand as a trainee in the morning. Our plan is to divide our time between London and Dream Valley until we marry and have a family of our own. We can't think of a better place to raise them and plan on moving there and setting up our own business in the most perfect place in the world.

Blake will make many more trips there over the coming months and I will travel with him, renting Rock House or a room at the guesthouse near Dreamy Sand beach. Sammy Jo and Marcus offered us a room at Valley House, but we decided it would be best if we kept our friendship, rather than take advantage of their hospitality.

"Eliza, darling, come and tell me what recipe you used to create these gorgeous vegan bites."

Julia's voice rings out loudly across the room of her stunning Wimbledon home and Blake nudges me and whispers, "Yes Eliza, do tell."

Throwing him a warning look, I turn and smile. "I would be delighted to, Julia. I'll text you the recipe."

Pretending to type it out, I merely forward the one Dorothy pinged me when I sent an SOS a few days ago. In fact, Dorothy Jenkins is my guru, and I cannot operate unless she gives me the go ahead. I am trying and have got way better domestically, but it pains me to say that Blake is much better than me in the kitchen.

We have enjoyed many evenings where I watch him cook while sipping the ever-present gin and tonic after a day at the office. I really think I have it all now and will be forever grateful to Annalise Turtle for nudging me in the direction of my dreams.

Blake sighs beside me and holds up his phone and I see a forwarded message from one of his friends with several laughing emojis added.

It's a post from Blake and Erin forever. When she was sent packing, she took on the role of the jilted lover and has spent the past few months posting about heartbreak and being dumped by the love of her life. Today's post reads,

What is stronger than the human heart, which shatters over and over and still lives? (Rupi Kaur)

My love for Blake (crying face emoji)

There's another one that follows.

Choosing me and my happiness has been the best decision and he will soon regret losing my heart.

(Broken heart emoji)

You were my cup of tea, but I drink cocktails now. *(Cocktail emoji)*

"Do you think she'll ever find anyone?"

I feel bad for her, and he shrugs. "I think she already did, look."

He scrolls up and I stare at a photograph of her with another man captioned,

New Beginnings are the best beginnings — together forever.

(7 heart emojis.)

"Do you think he knows they're an item?" I stare in horror at the picture of a man who looks a lot like Blake.

"Probably not. I hope so, though because I want her to find happiness, despite her crazy behaviour."

"You're a decent man, Blake Monroe. I doubt I'd be so forgiving."

"Yes, you would. I don't think it's in your nature to hold a grudge. You're just perfect."

He leans down and drops a light kiss on my lips and then I hear my father say loudly, "Did I ever tell you about the time I took Eliza to a sex shop?"

We spring apart and I groan, "Do something Blake, please!!!"

Laughing, Blake just smirks and walks towards them, saying over his shoulder, "This I have got to hear."

* * *

If you liked this story you may want to read Sammy Jo and Marcus' story in Coming home to Dream Valley.

If you missed Cruising in Love where Sammy Jo and Florrie meet the Hudson brothers, you can check it out here.
Cruising in Love

AFTER a happy ever disaster Florence heads off on her honeymoon cruise with her bridesmaid.

Hoping to enjoy two weeks of relaxation on an all-expenses-paid trip of a lifetime she was hoping to recharge and reflect on the cruel blow fate dealt her.

Her bridesmaid has other ideas and before she knows it, they are signed up to the ship's cruising in love programme where single passengers are paired up in a bid to find their shipmate.

Seven dates in seven days with a love match at the end and another week to get to know one another.

. . .

WILL it be love at first sight or an endless round of disastrous dates with nowhere to hide?

A light-hearted romance about starting again and discovering that everything happens for a very good reason.

* * *

Thank you for reading New Beginnings in Dream Valley.
If you liked it, I would love if you could leave me a <u>review</u>, as I must do all my own advertising.
This is the best way to encourage new readers and I appreciate every review I can get. Please also recommend it to your friends as word of mouth is the best form of advertising. It won't take longer than two minutes of your time, as you only need write one sentence if you want to.
NB: This book uses UK spelling.

Have you checked out my website? Subscribe to keep updated with any offers or new releases.

sjcrabb.com

WHEN YOU VISIT MY WEBSITE, you may be surprised because I don't just write Romantic comedy.

I also write under the pen names M J Hardy & Harper Adams. I send out a monthly newsletter with details of all my releases and any special offers but aside from that, you don't hear from me very often.

If you like social media, please follow me on mine where I am a lot more active and will always answer you if you reach out to me.

Why not take a look and see for yourself and read Lily's Lockdown, a little scene I wrote to remember the madness when the world stopped and took a deep breath?

Lily's Lockdown

More books by S J Crabb

The Diary of Madison Brown
My Perfect Life at Cornish Cottage
My Christmas Boyfriend
Jetsetters
More from Life
A Special Kind of Advent
Fooling in love
Will You
Holly Island
Aunt Daisy's Letter

The Wedding at the Castle of Dreams
My Christmas Romance
Escape to Happy Ever After
Cruising in Love
Coming Home to Dream Valley
Christmas in Dream Valley
New Beginnings in Dream Valley

sjcrabb.com

STAY IN TOUCH

You can also follow me on social media below.

Facebook

Instagram

Twitter

Website

Bookbub

Amazon

Printed in Great Britain
by Amazon

79761446R00120